TOKYO TORPEDO

U-BOAT SERIES BOOK THREE

EDWYN GRAY

WOLFPACK
PUBLISHING
— EST 2013 —

Tokyo Torpedo
U-Boat Series Book Three
Edwyn Gray

Print Edition
© Copyright 2018 (as revised) Edwyn Gray

Wolfpack Publishing
6032 Wheat Penny Avenue
Las Vegas, NV 89122

Paperback ISBN: 978-1-64119-382-5

Library of Congress Control Number: 2018958387

To Sue and Mark

As of today, I take over the post of Commander-in-Chief of the Navy, by order of the Fuhrer. I thank our submarine arm, which I have been permitted to command hitherto, for its death-defying readiness to fight that it has shown at all times and for its loyalty. I shall continue to retain command of the U-boats. I will command the Navy with the same hard, soldierly spirit. I expect from each one unconditional obedience, the highest courage, and devotion to the last. In that lies our honour. Gathered round our Fuhrer, we shall not lay down our arms until victory and peace have been achieved.

Order of the Day from Grossadmiral Karl Doenitz
(30th January 1943)

TOKYO TORPEDO

ONE

The overnight snow lying on the pavements of the Avenue Souchon and now melting into deep ruts of dirty brown slush was an ominous reminder that Germany's Eastern Front was in the freezing grip of the Russian winter. And as he glanced through the curtained windows of his office in the centre of Occupied Paris, Admiral Doenitz thought of General Paulus's encircled 6th Army outside Stalingrad.

Poor bastards! They'd lost all chance of survival when Hitler ordered them to stand firm in the face of the Russian pincers closing in to cut off their only hope of retreat. Now, frozen and shivering in sub-zero winds sweeping bleakly across the Steppes from the Arctic tundra of polar Russia, they lay crouched in shallow trenches that would soon be their graves. Blinded by driving blizzards, their breath freezing on their unshaven faces and burning deep into gaunt flesh already deadened and numbed by unrelenting frosts, they awaited death with disciplined stoicism.

Even the U-boat crews fighting for survival in the

teeth of raging North Atlantic gales - cold, wet and exhausted on their exposed conning towers with the ever-present threat of a choking death entombed in their iron coffins on the bottom of the ocean - were better off than their Wehrmacht comrades on the Eastern Front. And that, for Doenitz, was a significantly generous admission.

As the Admiral turned away from the window, he concluded, not for the first time, that the Fuhrer was mad. Everyone had warned him of the dangers of a winter campaign but he had persisted with the offensive and as a result of his blind obstinacy, the entire 6th Army was likely to be completely wiped out within a few days. And now, as if to compound his madness, the Fuhrer had ordered the big ships of the German Navy to be disarmed and hulked.

'Coastal Defence can make much better use of their guns than our "tin boxes" can - and our armament industry is crying out for scrap metal,' he had told Grossadmiral Raeder sarcastically at their historic confer-ence on 6 January 1943. And despite the C-in-C's warning that 'our enemy England, whose whole conduct of the war stands or falls by the control of the seas, would regard the war as good as won if Germany destroyed her ships', the Fuhrer had pursued his chosen objective with the inevitable result that Raeder tendered his resignation.

It was 29 January. And tomorrow Doenitz would be entering the OKM's headquarters on the Tirpitzufer in Berlin as the Navy's new Commander-in-Chief.

Yet even this change had caused friction between Hitler and the Kriegsmarine. Raeder had recommended Admiral Karls for the appointment but the Fuhrer, deter-mined to maintain his authority, had rejected the sugges-tion and picked instead the man who, as BdU, had led

Germany's U-boats in sinking 15 million tons of enemy shipping in just over four years of war. A man whose professional skill even the Fuhrer was forced to respect. And a man who had already proved his ability to achieve victory against all the odds.

Doenitz was understandably reluctant to leave his beloved submarines. At least in his Paris headquarters and at the Atlantic bases, he was safely many hundreds of miles away from Hitler and his crazy schemes. And when he had discussed the new organisation with Hitler, he had insisted on remaining as BdU while delegating day-to-day command of the U-boats to his trusted Chief of Staff, Rear Admiral Godt. Despite his promotion, Doenitz had no intention of releasing his grip on Germany's most powerful weapon - the U-boats.

But there were still eight hours left before the Heinkel 11 took off from Le Bourget to fly him to his new destiny at OKM. And to a man of Doenitz's energy, much could be accomplished in the space of eight hours.

There was certainly one matter he wanted to get out of the way before he left for Berlin. It had started as yet another of the Fuhrer's wild schemes dreamed up in a moment of pique and thrown at the Navy without thought to the practical problems involved. But Doenitz could discern a germ of usefulness in the idea and he was determined to push ahead with the scheme before Hitler changed his mind.

Japan had been Germany's ally in the Far East since that fateful Sunday morning in December 1941 when Admiral Nagumo's First Carrier Striking Force had hurled its aircraft at the American Pacific Fleet anchored snugly in Pearl Harbor. Communications between the two geographical extremes of the Tokyo-Rome-Berlin

Axis were difficult and physical contact virtually impossible. Both allies, fighting for the common cause of world domination, operated independently yet both needed the help of the other. Japan was desperately short of high-quality scientific equipment; Germany was starved of vital raw materials such as rubber and tin.

But of equal importance to these material requirements was the need for senior service officers and diplomats to meet their counterparts face to face to discuss problems of global strategy and the higher direction of war policy. And, of course, to agree on a division of the spoils when the two forces finally linked up in the Middle East - Germany driving eastwards through Egypt and Syria while the Japanese army swept triumphantly across the Indian sub-continent and Persia.

Such laudable considerations, however, were not uppermost in Hitler's mind when he first thought of sending a U-boat to Japan. In fact, his motivation was no higher than angry jealousy that Germany had not been first in the field.

The Japanese submarine I-30 had blazed the trail when, after an epic voyage from Singapore via the Cape of Good Hope, she had arrived at Lorient on 5 August 1942. And Hitler hated to be in second place to anyone. Doenitz remembered the occasion well. He had been amongst the Navy's top brass who greeted Commander Endo on his arrival in Europe and, on the Fuhrer's personal orders, decorated the Japanese submarine captain with a German medal.

And Doenitz, like Hitler, had shrewdly realised that I-30's historic visit was no empty propaganda gesture. The submarine had brought a valuable cargo of quinine with her and Endo's shopping list had included a request for German radar and radio equipment, Zeiss binoculars, and a host of precision scientific apparatus which Japan was incapable of manufacturing at home.

It was a pity, Doenitz thought wryly, that having returned safely to Singapore the unfortunate I-30 had been sunk by a British mine on the last leg of her return trip to Tokyo. But Endo had blazed the trail. And it was up to the Kriegsmarine to exploit it.

The Admiral began sifting through the pile of papers littering his desk and leaned back in his chair when he found the file he wanted. The more he thought about the idea the more attractive it became. Doenitz was not concerned with propaganda or trading penny-packets of war material. He saw it as an opportunity for spreading his U-boats into new and fruitful operational areas; of creating new danger zones that would stretch the Royal Navy's anti-submarine defences to breaking point. For the Admiral was a man with no illusions. No matter what victories the Wehrmacht might achieve or what damage the Luftwaffe inflicted on the enemy, Germany could not win the war until the British Navy was beaten. And only the U- boats were capable of inflicting such a defeat on Churchill's fleet.

The group of U-boats was already operating off the Cape and along the eastern coast of Africa but shortages of fuel were restricting their movements and even the milch-cows - the tanker submarines specially built to refill the empty bunkers of the long-range U-boats - had proved only partially successful. But with a shore base some-where in Malaysia - at Singapore, for example, or Penang - a flotilla of German submarines could virtually paralyse Allied shipping routes between India and Australia. Not to mention the vital tanker route from the Gulf.

But something else drew Doenitz's thoughts towards Japan. Something that, in the hands of the German Navy, could turn the tide of the war at sea almost overnight. And that something was the Long Lance torpedo - the weapon that had astounded the American Navy and which had contributed more than anything else to Japan's sweeping victories in the Pacific.

Beyond a shadow of a doubt, the Type-93 was the world's most secret torpedo. And it was a secret Doenitz was willing to pay any price for.

All official requests to Tokyo for details of the Long Lance had been met with brusque refusals. It seemed that the Japanese were not prepared to disclose the Type-93's secrets to anyone - not even their main ally. Yet Doenitz was convinced that a personal approach might yield results. And what better than a visit from a veteran U-boat ace to break the ice?

The Kriegsmarine's new C-in-C forced himself to stop daydreaming and looked down at the file spread open in front of him. He had already decided who was the best man to send on such a delicate mission. And he opened the file to refresh his memory of Kapitanleutnant Bergman's career:

IN CONFIDENCE
Form OKM-E/55
(Category B)

SUMMARY REPORT

NAME: Konrad Siegfried Bergman
   Rank: Kapitanleutnant
   Branch: Unterseeboot Flotille
   Date of Birth: 17 Mar 1916
   Seniority No: 654
   Appointment: Staff BdU

1. CAREER HISTORY

1932 – Cadet Flensburg Academy. Sword of Honour. Joint best cadet.

1934 – Sail training ship *Gorch Fock*. Grade AA report.

1935 – *Pommern* as junior watchkeeper. Grade A minus report.

1935 – Periscope School Kiel. Klass 3/36. 3rd in final examination.

February 1, 1933 To *UB-2* as Third Officer.

December 10, 1937 To *Emden* as senior watchkeeper.

August 1, 1938 To *UB-16* as Executive Officer. Special recommendation.

August 1, 1939 To *UB-44* in command. 10th Flotilla.

May 25, 1941 Graded unfit for sea duties following loss of *UB-44* in action. Special recuperative leave.

July 16, 1941 To OKM (Naval Intelligence) as senior assistant.

January 12, 1942 Seconded for duty at Fuhrer's HQ - Naval Section.

June 19, 1942 To Staff BdU as Assistant Operations Officer. Regraded fit for sea duty.

1. COMBAT RECORD

CONFIRMED   SINKINGS: 14   merchant   ships.
(140,398 BRT) HMS *Salisbury* (Cruiser)
   HMS *Stingray* (Submarine)
   HMS *Weasel* (Destroyer)
   3 enemy aircraft destroyed.
   9 combat patrols in command. North Sea, Arctic, N.
Atlantic and Gulf of Mexico.

1. DECORATIONS

IRON CROSS (2ND CLASS); Submarine Insignia;
Iron Cross (1st Class); Knights Cross of the Iron Cross.
Personal commendation by the Fuhrer for special services
to the Reich. (1940.)

1. NOTES

RECOMMENDED for combat sea duty in command.
Appointment as Flotilla Commander when seniority
appropriate.
   Personal reports: Grade AA. Confirmed by BdU.
Medical Category: AA-i.

DOENITZ SLIPPED the Summary Report back into the
sleeve of the blue establishment file. He was pleased to
see the AA-i grading on the last medical report. There
had been a time when, yielding to the stresses of
continual combat operations, Bergman's health had given

cause for anxiety. And the complete breakdown that followed the sinking of *UB-44* would have seen him invalided out of the Navy but for the C-in-C of U-boat's personal intervention. But the Kapitanleutnant had made an excellent recovery and, if anything, had even benefited from his experiences.

The snow had begun falling again but the Admiral was too deeply immersed in his work to notice it. Bent over his desk, he read methodically through the annual appraisal reports and jotted odd notes on a slip of paper in his distinctively angular writing. Slipping the last report back into the file, Doenitz leaned back in his chair and tapped his chin thoughtfully with a silver pencil. There was no need to check the other three files lying on the left-hand side of the desk waiting examination. Bergman was clearly the best man for the task.

But in addition to the bald statements of fact recorded in the file, there was something else which, in Doenitz's eyes, made the young Kapitanleutnant especially suitable for the delicate mission in mind. He was not a member of the Party. And that in itself was recommendation enough for the Admiral.

But what would Bergman's reaction be? Naturally he'd be delighted to get command of a U-boat again. But to be withdrawn from combat operations for a mission that promised to be more diplomatic than military - that was a different matter altogether. And Doenitz knew from experience that Bergman was not the easiest of men to persuade. In fact, despite his reputation for unquestioned obedience to orders, the Kapitanleutnant had developed an uneasy knack of doing precisely what he wanted to do without, so it seemed, deviating from the task originally set. And Doenitz had little doubt that even if Bergman accepted his offer of the Japanese mission something unusual - and probably valuable - would come out of it.

Having prepared himself, Doenitz called up the Duty Officer in the next room and told him to fetch Bergman from the Operations Room. Then, lighting a cigarette, the Admiral sat staring out of the window at the falling snow.

Kapitanleutnant Bergman had changed little since his first interview with the C-in-C of U-boats on the day Germany had invaded Poland and started the war. A few extra lines around his eyes, a harder set to his mouth, and a hint of grey in the dark hair of his temples. But otherwise as alert as ever with an inner strength of character that could be felt rather than seen. Not even the trauma of losing his boat and ninety percent of his crew had left any visible marks on him. And the strain of nine hard-fought combat patrols sat lightly on his broad shoulders.

'Come in, Bergman.' The Admiral waved towards one of the leather armchairs facing his solid oak desk. 'Sit down and make yourself comfortable.'

'Thank you, sir.'

Bergman showed no sign of awe in the presence of his Commander-in-Chief. Like most U-boat commanders, he was familiar with the austerely-furnished office and on friendly terms with the grey-eyed Admiral who guided his destiny and who, one day, would guide the destiny of Germany itself. It was standard practice for Doenitz to have a personal chat with his U-boat captains both before and after patrols and Bergman regarded the invitation as normal routine.

'Are you fit enough for a sea command again?' Doenitz knew the Medical Board's rating but he was shrewd enough to want Bergman's personal opinion. A great deal could be read into a man's answer when you were experienced in such matters. And he had no high opinion of the Kriegsmarine doctors in any case.

'Yes, sir.' Bergman committed himself no further. He, too, knew the Medical Board's verdict. But these days he tended to be uncommunicative as if his private thoughts and opinions were his personal property. And it was difficult enough to hide feelings in today's Germany with the SS and the Gestapo listening at every door.

'You don't sound very sure, Kapitanleutnant.' Doenitz probed for the weak spot like a skilled fencer sizing up an unknown opponent.

'I'm quite sure, sir. A spell of sea duty would probably do me good after sitting around on my butt so long.' His mouth turned down sardonically. 'And I've got a few old debts to pay off ...'

Doenitz nodded. He knew this was a reference to the sinking of *UB-44* but he let it pass without comment. No point in stirring up old wounds. Most skippers took the loss of their ship to heart.

'It won't be the Atlantic this time.' He watched Bergman's face intently and was slightly disappointed by the lack of reaction. 'This is a special mission.'

Bergman's guts suddenly churned and he felt his hands sweating as he recalled the last special mission he had undertaken. Good God, not *that* again. Hiding the fear from his face, he nodded. After all, even Doenitz was unaware of *UB-44*'s part in the destruction of the pocket-battleship *Koenig*. And the only man who could have betrayed the secret, Herzog, the coxswain of *UB-44*, now lay dead on the bottom of the Atlantic.

'Where to, sir?'

'Japan.'

Bergman's mask of indifference vanished. Despite his outward calm, his pulse raced with excitement. The Far East and Japan had always held a fascination for him and the opportunity of going there while the war was still on was an unexpected gift from the gods. And of equal importance to his personal desires, it would put an insurmountable barrier between himself and the Gestapo. But then, like the *Koenig* incident, Doenitz was also unaware of his brush with Gruppenfuhrer Gorst in Lorient.

'But the special mission, sir? What am I supposed to do - sink the American Pacific fleet on my own to keep us one up on the Japs?'

The Admiral smiled and shook his head. 'Not quite, Bergman. Although I have no doubt that you'd try if I let you. Officially, you will be testing the feasibility of a regular U-boat shuttle service between Europe and Japan. And finding a suitable base from which we can operate a combat flotilla in the Indian Ocean.' He stood up and walked across to a large wall chart of the Far East. 'At present,' he explained, indicating the coastline of East Africa, 'we can only operate our submarines up as far as Madagascar. And we can only maintain them on station by feeding them with fuel and torpedoes from the new supply U-boats we have built specifically for that purpose. The British have realised what we are up to and they're making a special point of attacking our supply boats with the result that we can no longer maintain our patrol lines and I have had to withdraw all U-boats westwards into the South Atlantic.'

'But couldn't we use the French African bases - Madagascar or one of the smaller islands like Reunion? I can't see Petain or Laval raising any objections.'

Doenitz sighed. 'Of course, I forgot you do not have

access to the latest war situation. It's no use reading the newspapers these days - the German people only get told what the Propaganda Ministry wants them to know. The answer to your suggestion is simply that the British have beaten us to it. They attacked Diego Suarez in May last year and forced the French authorities to capitulate - the French seem to have a propensity for losing wars these days. But the Vichy regime started their usual double-cross game and a British task force invaded the island again about three months ago.' He paused for a moment and grinned. 'I needn't add that the French surrendered.'

Bergman had heard rumours of the Madagascar affair but even at U-boat headquarters, hard facts outside the immediate sphere of their own operations were hard to find. As Doenitz said quite rightly, the German people didn't know the half of it.

'What is your suggestion then, sir?'

The Admiral studied the map thoughtfully and moved his finger to the north of Singapore and along the western coastline of the Malay peninsula.

'My first choice would be Penang Island and so far as our diplomats can ascertain, it's the only place the Japanese are likely to let us use. But you might find some-where else more suitable.'

'Wasn't Penang the place von Muller bombarded with *Emden* in 1914?'

Doenitz smiled. That was what he liked about Bergman. He knew his history. And to a Navy as new as the Kriegsmarine where tradition was lacking, he looked to men like the Kapitanleutnant to create it.

'I congratulate you on your memory, Bergman. Let us hope von Muller's success will be an omen for the future. I must remember to remind the Fuhrer of that particular episode next time he runs down the Navy's part in the last war.' He chuckled at the thought. 'So that's the first part of your task, Kapitanleutnant. Find a suitable base in the Indian Ocean for a U-boat flotilla.'

'And the other part, Herr Admiral?' Bergman reminded him.

'Ah, yes. I had almost forgotten. The Japanese seem very reluctant to supply us with details of their new Long Lance torpedo - I'm sure you have heard about its exploits against the Americans.' Bergman nodded. 'Well, I want you to continue on to Japan after leaving Penang. Tokyo will be advised of your arrival. And when you get there, I want you to try and get the full technical details of the torpedo. So far the Japanese have refused to tell us anything but I am certain in my own mind that a personal approach will yield the desired results. And if anyone can persuade the Tokyo admirals to pass over the plans, it will be you. So, as far as I am concerned, the *Type-93* is the *real* purpose of your mission.'

The Kapitanleutnant stood up. 'I understand, sir.'

'I hope you do,' Doenitz observed drily. 'And remember - I want no underhand tricks and no spying. If you cannot persuade them to pass over the plans freely, that will be the end of the matter.'

'Sir.'

Doenitz glanced down at the papers on his desk. Well, that was that. He had settled the Far East matter and Bergman was back on combat duty. Now he had exactly seven hours and twenty-one minutes to settle the other hundred-and-one problems lying on his desk before flying to Berlin to take over as the Kriegsmarine's new Commander-in-Chief.

'I'm afraid there has been insufficient time to allow

you to select your own crew,' he explained apologetically. 'But you have my assurance they have all been hand-picked for the task. Your boat will be *U-885* - one of our latest *Type IXD(2)* submarines. You'll find her a consider-able improvement over the old *UB-44*. Oberleutnant von Schroeder, the Executive Officer, has already brought her down to Lorient from the Germania works at Kiel and she's been thoroughly worked up and tested in the Baltic with Eighteen Flotilla. How soon can you get away?'

'By this evening, sir. I always keep a spare suitcase packed.'

'Excellent. Now if you will report to the Director of Operations, he will brief you on the mission and hand over your written orders. And remember. A great deal depends on the results of this mission and I am relying on you.' Doenitz stood up and held out his hand. 'Good luck, Bergman.'

The Kapitanleutnant grasped the outstretched hand firmly and then, replacing his cap, he snapped to attention and saluted.

KOMMODORE SCHILLER WAS in an expansive mood. But then he usually was and even in the worst moments of crisis, it was rare to see his face without a smile. Bluff, genial, and tending to obesity, he looked more like a benevolent retired admiral than Doenitz's Director of Operations but Bergman knew him well enough to appreciate the steel determination behind the smiling mask. Schiller, for all his outward geniality, was tough and ruthless. And although basically different in character, the two men each recognised a little of themselves in the other so, despite a mutual respect, they treated each other warily like two battle-scarred lions circling carefully before combat.

'Come in, Konrad. Good to see you!' Schiller waved a plump hand towards the armchair alongside his desk. 'Take a seat. Cigar?'

Bergman shook his head as the Kommodore pushed the silver box towards him.

'I presume the Grossadmiral has told you the outline of your mission,' Schiller observed casually through a cloud of blue cigar smoke. 'And note, I said outline.'

'Yes, sir. I am to take U-885 to Japan via Malaya.'

'And?' Schiller prompted.

'I am to locate a suitable base for an operational flotilla in the Indian Ocean. The Admiral has also instructed me to negotiate with the Japanese and obtain the plans and details of the Type-93 torpedo.'

Schiller laughed. 'Typical of the Old Man,' he chuckled as if enjoying a personal joke. 'Typical. That's the worst of having a gentleman in command of the Navy.' He looked up sharply. 'Can you really imagine these Tokyo bastards giving us the Long Lance plans on a plate just by asking nicely?'

'I really don't know, Herr Kommodore,' Bergman shrugged. He respected Doenitz's integrity and was irritated by Schiller's sneering sarcasm. It was well known that the Kommodore had only won promotion by virtue of his membership of the Nazi Party and the Kapitanleutnant resented his key position in the U-boat arm.

'Well, I'll tell you. They won't! And Doenitz is a fool if he thinks they will. The Japs are a secretive load of bastards. The only way we'll get hold of those plans is to steal them. And that's exactly why you're being sent on this mission.'

'But the Admiral specifically forbade...'

'You will steal the plans, Bergman. And that's an order.'

'Supposing Admiral Doenitz finds out?'

'He won't. Once he's safely in Berlin, he'll be too cut off to follow the details of our U-boat operations.' Schiller smiled. 'And there's another reason. All reports and information are channelled through this office. And *I* shall ensure that Doenitz hears only what I want him to hear.'

Bergman kept his mouth tightly shut. He had come to learn a great deal about the politics of the U-boat service during his period of staff work and as a combat officer, he had no intention of becoming involved in the continual struggle for power. And now that Doenitz was destined for Berlin there was no opportunity of warning him. The Kapitanleutnant shivered. It was the *Koenig* situation all over again. And he was the fall guy as usual. Well, he had learned to look after his own interests since then and this was the moment when he must play it cautiously.

What happened when he finally reached Japan was a matter between himself and his conscience. He might play it Schiller's way - or he might obey Doenitz's instructions. Whatever happened, he would make the decision himself and to hell with the consequences. So far as Bergman was concerned, the days of carrying out orders in blind obedience were over and gone forever.

'And if I get caught?' he asked the Kommodore.

'We shall disown you, of course,' Schiller chuckled. 'Don't forget that the Grossadmiral himself warned you to do nothing underhanded.' His rotund face was suddenly and unexpectedly serious. It was the first time Bergman had seen him without a smile in all the years they had served together. 'But you *won't* get caught, Konrad. If I thought there was even the smallest danger, I would never have suggested it.' He leaned forward confidentially. 'The Fuhrer personally selected you for this mission when I explained the plan. As you probably know, he has had his eye on you for some time. It was a simple matter to feed Doenitz a specially prepared short-list that guaranteed your selection.'

Bergman suddenly realised that the mission could be a one-way ticket. Schiller had engineered the entire scheme - probably even sowing the first seed of the torpedo idea in Doenitz's mind. And if Hitler had personally selected him for the Far East trip, there were only two possible reasons. First, because after the *Koenig* affair, he thought Bergman was ruthless enough to succeed. Or, secondly and more probably, it was part of a deeper plan for the Kapitanleut-nant to be eliminated and dishonoured. His period of service on the Fuhrer's staff had developed a cynicism that was alien to Bergman's character and he had little doubt that the second alternative was the more likely. It would be an easy matter to arrange for him to get caught red-handed.

His expression gave no hint of the thoughts flashing through his mind. On the contrary, there was an eager-ness in his face that gave the impression he was more than willing to take up the challenge. And he maintained the lie in a calmly quiet voice.

'I'll do my best, Herr Kommodore. I will try the Admi-ral's way but if that doesn't work ...' He left the sentence uncompleted in a silent unspoken promise.

Schiller beamed.

'There is only one other point, sir,' Bergman contin-ued. 'How many people know the details of the mission?'

'Why? Want to disappear for a few months, Konrad?'

Schiller laughed at the thought. 'Got one of your girl-friends in the family way, I suppose. Want to get away until it's all over.'

Bergman's reasons for wanting to escape from Europe were his own. And he had no intention of telling the Kommodore what they were. But if that was what he wanted to think - well, let him.

'Something like that, sir. Only it's a bit more complicated.'

Schiller slapped his thigh and bellowed with amusement. 'Not two?'

The Kapitanleutnant contrived to look suitably abashed but he carefully avoided meeting the Kommodore's eyes.

'Don't worry, Bergman. You'll be perfectly safe. Apart from the Grossadmiral and the Fuhrer, nobody outside these four walls knows where you are going - not even my staff nor the crew of *U-885*.'

A FEW BLOCKS away in a small office at the Gestapo Headquarter's building in the Avenue Foch, Gruppen-fuhrer Gorst put down the telephone.

'So my friend Kapitanleutnant Bergman is going to Japan . . . now that could lead to a very interesting situation.' His voice, a hoarse whisper as the result of a throat wound during a beer-garden brawl in the days before the Munich *putsch,* hissed like a sibilant snake as he spoke his thoughts. Neisser, his assistant, looked up from yesterday's edition of *Das Schwarze Korps.*

'Bergman?'

Gorst stabbed the sharply pointed paperknife into the top of his desk with a vicious jab.

'Yes - Bergman. You're too new to know about him but you'll find his dossier in the Reichsfuhrer's personal archives.'

Neisser was suitably impressed. A product of the Hitler Youth and the SS leadership school at Bad-Tolz, he was still feeling his way through the labyrinth channels of the Gestapo. But he was already experienced enough to know that anyone who qualified for a dossier in Himmler's personal office must be very important; at the very least, an enemy of the state to be eliminated at the earliest opportunity.

'A naval officer?'

'A U-boat captain to be precise. And the man responsible for having me sent to the Eastern Front with the 19th SS Panzer Battalion. I'll never forgive him for that.' Gorst held up the maimed remnants of his left hand where frostbite had eaten deeply through flesh and bone. 'And if I hadn't been lucky, I'd be there still.'

'What happened?' Neisser asked the question timorously. He was still frightened of Gorst.

The Gruppenfuhrer embroidered the truth. He had no intention of admitting that Bergman had outsmarted him. And the defeat still rankled.

'If it had not been for Kapitanleutnant Bergman, the SS would now have full powers of arrest over any officer or man of the armed forces. I had it all sewn up - the bait, the situation, and the evidence. And then that bastard Bergman murdered one of my best operatives in Lorient and the whole case fell to pieces.'

Neisser nodded. He'd heard colourful rumours of the Lorient affair when he had first arrived at the Paris office but he had taken little notice of them. The Gestapo, he had discovered, was fond of malicious gossip. But this particular man had apparently really got under the Gruppenfuhrer's skin. He closed the magazine and tossed it onto his desk.

'Well, if this Bergman character's off to Japan, it'll get him out of our hair for a few months. Give us time to finish infiltrating that resistance group in the Ardennes. I've got some ideas about how ...'

Gorst was not listening. Leaning his elbows on the desk, he rubbed his chin thoughtfully as he considered the latest turn of events.

'He'll think he's safe once he gets out East - lower his guard,' he whispered, thinking out loud. 'I haven't been able to get near him since I got back from Stalingrad. But now we've got a chance.'

'But the Reichsfuhrer SS won't permit you to go out to Japan,' Neisser pointed out. 'And if you stay here in Europe, how are you going to do anything to him?'

Gorst smiled and the stumped fingers of his left hand began drumming the desk top rhythmically. 'I can do nothing,' he agreed. 'But fortunately we have excellent links with the Kempei Tai. Our agent in Lisbon can get a message out to Colonel Shikura in Tokyo. Just a gentle warning, you understand. And Shikura or one of his men will arrange an accident. Unfortunate, of course - German U-boat hero killed by non-stop car in Far East. But it will be too bloody far away for any of the Kriegsmarine people to check on. And if they do, I can rely on Shikura to block their inquiries.'

He paused and Neisser could see him staring at the wall deep in thought.

'A pfennig for them,' he offered out of curiosity.

Gorst tilted his chair back and transferred his gaze to the ceiling. He disliked sharing his thoughts with anyone. But his senses were tuned to detect the fractional shades of behaviour that often yielded a clue to more vital matters and he felt impelled to share them with someone. Even, he thought contemptuously, that *kleine votze,* Neisser.

'I wonder why Bergman's really going out to Japan. If we knew that, it would make matters easier for Shikura. I'm damned sure there's some dirty business involved somewhere along the line. And that's why they've picked Bergman for the job.' He leaned forward across the desk with sudden decision and his hoarse whisper rose in pitch. 'We're going to be very busy, Neisser. We need to know more about Bergman's mission - a lot more!'

TWO

Resting his arms on the lip of the bridge coaming, Bergman clasped his hands together and stared towards the bows as *U-885* swung onto an easterly course. Diamond Point slipped astern and the sharp tang of sea air smelled fresh and sweet after the fetid stink of the mangroves. The U-boat had been hugging the shoal waters of the Sumatran coast for the last hundred miles and the heady scent of rotting vegetation carried seaward by a breeze blowing off the land still hung heavily over the submarine.

On deck, the humid heat was bad enough. But below in the airless vault of the narrow hull, it was unadulterated hell. Not even *U-885*'s powerful fans could stir life into the sluggish air and the torpid atmosphere was not improved by the constant drip of condensated moisture running down the inner plating. The temperature stood at 110° and aside from a brief spell off-duty for the lucky ones on deck, there was no respite from the stamina-sapping heat and humidity.

'Now I know how those poor bloody sausages feel

when Schmidt's frying them in the galley,' Brecht grumbled as he lay in his bunk reading a tattered copy of the Olympia Press's latest book which one of his friends had bought in Paris a few weeks earlier.

No one laughed. He'd said the same thing with monotonous regularity every day for the past three weeks. And most of the men had long passed their threshold of tolerance for inane remarks.

Willi Hartman, the occupier of the upper berth, lifted himself up on one elbow and wiped the sweat from his face. He was completely naked and his thin body and pallid skin looked like a caricature of a living skeleton.

'How far now?'

Manhaussen chewed his thumb as he considered the question. As a former *hochskool* student, the men usually looked to him for answers.

'A day - maybe a couple.' He shrugged. 'Depends on where the skipper decides to put in. Could be Singapore or Java. Perhaps further up the coast.'

'How the hell do you know?' Brecht sneered from behind his book. 'Just because the Executive Officer lets you play around with the charts...' He paused. 'Or does he play around with you?'

Manhaussen's face darkened at the insinuation but he bit back his temper. One day he'd be a U-boat officer - he was an ambitious young man - and when that day came, he'd deal with Brecht. But until then he had to keep his nose clean and make a good impression. The others knew it and they exploited their knowledge.

Willi Hartmann rolled over onto his back and stared up at the moisture trickling down the sweating bulkhead that curved less than two feet above his bunk.

'Java ... I saw it at a news cinema once. That's the

place where the girls walk around with their tits on show. Christ! Tell the skipper to get a move on. I can't wait.'

'That's Bali, you randy bastard. But they tell me there's plenty of tit about in Malaya, too,' Schmidt's eyes gleamed and he licked his dry lips with anticipation, 'especially when they're having their daily wash in the river.'

Brecht clawed his hand upwards and clasped the steel tube running along the base of Hartmann's bunk. His bicep bulged under the weight of his body and he hauled himself upwards to peer over the edge of the mattress.

'Dirty little sod,' he jeered gleefully. 'That's what comes of you bastards talking about tits - no wonder the Old Man makes us keep our pants on. Gives the game away, don't it, Willi?' He turned to the others sitting round the bare wooden mess table that filled the middle of the forward torpedo compartment. 'Hey, you guys, come and take a look at what Willi's got!'

There was a mad scramble and a hoot of laughter as Hartmann quickly grabbed a towel and rolled over to hide his embarrassment.

Manhaussen intervened to keep the peace. 'Lay off the kid.' The fact that he was barely nineteen years old himself was of small consequence. But the narrow insignia on his sleeve gave him the necessary authority. Franz was proud of the little stripe. It was the first rung on the ladder to his ultimate ambition and he enjoyed the precarious seniority it gave him over the others members of the fore-ends mess. 'Put your pants on, Hartmann,' he admonished sharply. 'You know the Captain's orders about minimum off-duty rig. And if the rest of you have nothing to do, you can start cleaning up this pigsty! '

Diamond Point had disappeared astern as eight bells

tolled the end of the Forenoon Watch and U-885 struck out across the narrow waters of the Malacca Strait on the last leg of her journey to Penang. Her shark-shaped bows dipped gracefully into the southerly swell and a refreshing whisper of spray helped to soothe the men standing watch under the burning disc of the noon sun.

So far, they'd enjoyed a quiet trip. And thank the Lord for small mercies thought Bergman. At least it had given him time to get to know his boat and his crew even though the knowledge he had acquired was not very reassuring. What had Doenitz promised - a handpicked crew? But handpicked for what? The Grossadmiral had conveniently forgotten to tell him that.

To begin with, most of the men were conscripts. Not that Bergman held them to blame for that. No sane man would volunteer for U-boat service these days. But of all the men he had encountered during his eight years of service in the Kriegsmarine, U-885's crew were the most slovenly, useless and undisciplined bunch he had ever had the misfortune to meet. Some of them weren't even fit for service in an SS labour battalion. Their drills - and he had exercised them mercilessly during the outward passage - were still seconds behind his minimum expectations and no amount of exhortation, punishments, or cajolery had any effect on them. They would have been the despair of any self-respecting U-boat commander but to a man like Bergman, accustomed to the highest standards and needing a taut crew to face the dangers that lay ahead, their sullen lack of interest and enthusiasm was scarcely a good omen for the success of the mission.

Not that they were all bad. Schwarze, for example, was keen enough and so was Mueller. And young Manhaussen looked a hopeful prospect if his morale were not undermined by the corruptness of his mess-mates in the forward torpedo compartment. That was always the danger, that men like Hartmann and Brecht would spread the contagion of slovenliness and indiscipline amongst the more reliable hands. And in the confined space of an operational U-boat, it was all too easy. Cramped quarters and boredom, hours of aimless mechanical duties, and the sapping debility of the humid heat of the tropics were an ideal breeding ground for disaffection.

And then there was Bottcher. Not one of the young conscripts, that one, but an old hand from the pre-war Navy. Bergman considered that he'd never seen Bottcher do a stroke of work since the day they'd left Lorient. He was either sick, off-duty, about to go on duty, or excused duty by some other officer. Yet he, of all people, should have been the mainstay of the inexperienced younger members of the crew. But was he? Hell!

At least, Bergman decided with malicious satisfaction, the men were frightened of their skipper. Perhaps not so much of him personally for, with a long and tedious mission in prospect, he had had very little contact with them. But they certainly knew of his reputation.

Bergman had no illusions about himself. He knew he was not popular and he knew that he had a deserved reputation for ruthlessness. But the time had long passed when he worried about other people's opinions. The fact that his crew respected him was enough. And he was well aware that, for all their disaffection, every man aboard *U-885* grudgingly admitted that Kapitanleutnant Bergman would not let them down when the crunch came.

His mouth twisted cynically at the thought. Perhaps it was a good thing the secrets of his old boat *UB-44* had died with her on her final plunge to the bottom.

Still there was some sober reason for optimism. The last diving exercises had shown a little improvement and he had noted a new enthusiasm during gun-drill yesterday. Perhaps once they faced danger for the first time, when they realised that their survival depended on disciplined teamwork and that even a moment's carelessness by one single man could hazard the entire boat, they would finally find themselves. And if they didn't? He shrugged his shoulders despondently. Then, in that case, they'd all be dead the sooner. And in his darker moments, it was a fate he almost welcomed.

Bergman pushed himself reluctantly upright and walked across to cheek the gyro repeater. Course 120 and steady. He nodded.

'Checked against magnetic at 12-15, sir.'

Leutnant z.s. Teschen was Officer of the Watch and as a recent graduate of the Periscope School at Kiel, he was still bustingly over-zealous. This was only his second operational patrol and he was very conscious of his responsibilities.

'Very good, Teschen. And the men?'

'Sir?'

'Have you checked the men also?'

The young officer looked flustered. It seemed a stupid question but he did not dare say so to Bergman's face. Despite the gold ring on his sleeve, he was probably more terrified of the skipper than anyone else aboard. Of course he'd checked the men - it was impossible not to. There were only four of them on the bridge, one standing at each quarter, keeping lookout through their powerful binoculars. A long slow sweep across their allotted sector of the horizon. Then upwards to scan the high arc of the sky for aircraft before dropping down again for a repetition of the surface sweep.

It was a monotonous and boring task. After a few minutes, the eyes smarted; after five, they ached and within ten, the arm muscles were creaking in sympathy. There was never anything to see but Bergman would not allow them to relax their vigilance for a single second. It was the futility of the thing that made it most unbearable.

'Yes, sir,' Teschen faltered. 'They're at their stations.'

'I said *checked,* Herr Leutnant. Not looked at.' Bergman nodded towards the portly indolence of Bottcher keeping watch at the aft starboard quarter station. With *U-885* standing to the east, it was a veritable sun-trap and Bottcher's bulky body had an indefinable air of peaceful relaxation about it. Facing directly into the sun, he was not required to search the highest arc of sky - if an aircraft dived out of the sun it was a chance they had to take. His task was to search only the surface horizon and $45°$ above it. It was a restriction that Bottcher welcomed. At least it was one way of avoiding arm-ache.

Bergman said nothing but walked quietly aft until he was standing alongside the lookout. Then, stretching out his hand, he passed his fingers in front of the lenses.

There was no reaction from Bottcher. He continued his slow routine sweep of the horizon and the glasses tilted upwards as he moved his wrists to scan the sky sector. It was like a blind man carrying out some mystic ritual of worship - unseeing yet totally automatic from constant repetition. And it was obvious that, hidden behind the binoculars, Bottcher's eyes were closed and that he was snoozing peacefully in the sun while maintaining his pose of alert watchfulness.

Bergman wanted to kick him hard or do something

equally violent. Bottcher's guile could have placed the entire boat in danger. While the other three lookouts kept watch on their sectors, the southeast quadrant - the most dangerous area since any enemy attack would most likely take place out of the sun - was totally unguarded. And while Bottcher dozed, no one was keeping watch for the whisper of spray from an enemy periscope or the sudden telltale gleam of an aircraft's wings reflecting in the sun. U-885's skipper somehow kept a grip on his temper.

'Bottcher!'

The lookout jerked out of his catnap as Bergman's voice grated loudly in his ear. The binoculars dropped from his face and his eyes, still heavy with sleep, blinked nervously.

'Sorry, sir. Must have been the breakfast Schmidt served up this morning. Too heavy. Did I drop off?'

Bottcher had learned long ago that instant admission was probably the safest way to escape the inevitable retribution that flowed from neglect of duty. It took the sting out of the reprimand and caught his accuser off-guard. But he knew he had met his match with Bergman and the knowledge made his small pig-like eyes blink nervously as he stood rigidly to attention.

'I could have you shot!' Bergman's eyes were hard and cold. 'Sleeping on duty in the face of the enemy is a capital offence. And you know it! '

The lookout swallowed hard and tried to control the tremor that had seized his limbs. Christ! And the bastard would do it, too! Bergman's reputation was well-known in the U-boat service and Bottcher had inevitably heard only the more lurid aspects. Deciding that discretion was the better part of valour, he made no attempt to answer but stared fixedly out over the green-grey sea like a carved stone statue.

The Kapitanleutnant looked at him in silence for a few moments. Then, with sudden decision, he turned to the ashen-faced Teschen who was waiting uneasily at the rear.

'By God, I think I will!' he snapped. 'Fetch the Executive Officer to the bridge, Herr Leutnant. And I want two men topsides - with machine guns.'

Teschen stared at the skipper in disbelief. His mouth opened slackly but he could not find the right words.

'At the double, Herr Leutnant!'

'Sir!'

Teschen swung round and hurried to the voicepipe linking the bridge to the control room. His hands were shaking as he ripped off the lid and there was an uncontrollable tremor in his voice.

'Oberleutnant Schroeder to the bridge. Send up two men with automatic weapons. Captain's orders,' he added half-apologetically as if denying any responsibility for the command he was relaying.

Von Schroeder's head emerged through the conning-tower hatch almost immediately and the grim expression on his face reflected his fears. Heaving himself swiftly onto the bridge, he clicked his heels and saluted. Two of U-885's petty officers were behind him - Thyssen and Verlag, the bully-boys of the crew. And each cradled a Schmeisser submachine gun lovingly in his arms. Teschen's white face was now almost green with horror.

'You are familiar with operational instructions, Herr Oberleutnant?'

Von Schroeder nodded. 'I am, sir.'

'And the punishment for a man discovered asleep in the face of the enemy when he is on guard duties?'

'Yes, sir.'

'What are they?'

Von Schroeder needed no crystal ball to guess what had happened. It had been in the cards for a long time and he knew what the skipper was leading up to. But like Bergman, he had been brought up in the hard school of war and he made no attempt to shirk his responsibilities. He paused for a moment as if to mentally check his recollection of the relevant OKM order.

'Summary trial. Corroborative evidence by two officers. Execution.'

'Correct, Herr Oberleutnant.' Bergman turned to the young officer in the background. 'And do you confirm my evidence that the prisoner, Gefreiter Bottcher, was asleep while on duty?'

Teschen swallowed and glanced at the accused lookout. He felt as if he was passing sentence of death.

'Yes, sir. Gefreiter Bottcher appeared to be asleep. But...

'Yes, Herr Leutnant? You wish to add something?'

U-885's captain watched the young officer closely as he quietly thought about the challenge. For the first time in his life, Teschen was faced with the literal responsibility of a man's career. Bergman wondered how he would shape up to the test. Would he have the guts to face out his Commanding Officer and yet retain sufficient judgement to keep on the right side of the rules? 'Well, Herr Leutnant?'

'I agree Bottcher was asleep on duty, sir. But in my view, he was not asleep in the face of the enemy. The

President's findings in the court-martial of Natterheim distinguished the two offences - it was one of the cases we had to read for naval law at the Academy.'

Good for you, boy, Bergman thought to himself. You're not afraid to stand by your judgement but you've got the good sense to play it by the rules. Not that it made any difference but he had forgotten the Natterheim case.

Von Schroeder watched both men and waited. He'd had his reservations about young Teschen. Too young and soft to manage a bunch of hard-bitten U-boat men. But perhaps he had spunk in him after all. Somehow he felt it was Teschen who was being tried rather than Bottcher. Bergman might be utterly ruthless but he had never, to his knowledge, gunned a man down for a breach of discipline. And sensing the trial of strength being played out on the narrow bridge, he metaphorically stood to one side to watch the scene from the remote viewpoint of an impartial observer.

Bottcher, however, was in no fit state to consider the proceedings objectively. So far as he was concerned, he was in it up to his neck. His guts had turned to water and he could feel a growing wet patch in the crotch of his trousers as death stalked inexorably closer. That bastard Bergman would do it; have him gunned down for a minor offence just as an example to the others. He knew the Old Man had hated him from the moment he had reported for duty two hours late. And that stupid little *votze* Teschen was only making it worse. The more he riled the skipper, the more likely Bergman would order a summary execution to maintain his authority. Christ! Wasn't there any bloody justice on this stinking boat?

'We are in the face of the enemy, *Herr Leutnant*,' Bergman pointed out firmly. 'A U-boat is surrounded by enemies from the moment it leaves its base until the moment it returns. There is never a second when we are not facing instant danger and destruction.' He turned angrily on the lookout. 'And it's thanks to fools like him that many U-boats never return to their base.'

'I appreciate your view, sir. But I do not think the OKM order visualised this type of situation. However, I have given you my evidence. The ultimate decision must remain your responsibility as Commanding Officer.'

Touche. A neat little lesson in how to tell your skipper he's in the wrong without saying so directly. Bergman appreciated Teschen's tact. He wished he had shown similar diplomacy in the days when he had been serving as a subordinate officer. Still, as Teschen had pointed out, it was his decision. And although he had never really intended to go through with his threat, Bergman now had to extricate himself from the brink without loss of face. It would have been easier without Teschen's intervention. If he went back on his commitment now, there was a danger of the crew seeing it as weakness.

Bergman was aware that all eyes were on him as he considered his verdict. The two officers were both undoubtedly curious to see how he would handle an awkward situation. And those two sadists, Thyssen and Verlag, were obviously praying for an opportunity of using their guns on a defenceless victim. And Bottcher? His puffy face was sheet-white and, every few seconds his heavy body twitched with an uncontrollable tremor as the last moments of his life ticked away.

'Aircraft!'

The warning shout came from Siess, the port bow lookout. Bergman turned quickly.

'Where away?'

'Fine on the port bow, sir. About eight thousand feet.'

Bergman swore. Siess should have called off the bearing with his first warning. The question and answer wasted valuable seconds. But bored and inattentive, and probably listening to the dialogue on the lower bridge, he had forgotten the rules in the excitement of the sighting.

U-885's temperamental air-warning *Hohentwiel* radar had been out of service ever since the gale-force storm two days out from Lorient. But why hadn't Schwarze picked up the aircraft's radar pulses on his *Metox?* Was everyone trying to commit suicide?

The aircraft was still no more than a pinpoint above the horizon but Bergman's powerful Zeiss binoculars quickly defined it as a float-plane of unfamiliar type. And as he brought the tiny black dot into focus, von Schroeder hurried to the conning-tower hatch and slid down the ladder to take up his attack station in the control room.

'Stand by diving stations! All hands clear the bridge!'

U-boat training allocated precisely one and one-fifth seconds for each man to get down the narrow steel ladder. It was a matter of falling rather than descending and two men were kept posted at the foot of the ladder to assist. Squashed fingers and bruised faces were a normal reward for the effort involved.

Bottcher, moving like a man in a dream despite his bulk, was still half unable to grasp his unexpected reprieve as the diving alarm clamoured its strident warning and in his hurry to clear the bridge and escape the skipper's wrath, his feet slipped on the narrow steel rungs. He crashed down like a runaway elephant to a chorus of curses from Thyssen and Verlag who, descending the ladder below him, took the impact of his weight. All three men fell in a tangled swearing heap on the hard deck at the bottom of the ladder and Thyssen's machine gun clattered noisily across the steel plating.

Insults and threats brewed hotly and it needed the personal intervention of Oberbootsmann Kosch to restore order. Thrusting Bottcher through the watertight door towards the fore-ends, he curtly ordered the other two men to clear the control room and move aft. Thyssen picked up his gun and spat on the deck.

'Just wait till the skipper gives the word, Bottcher. I'm going to enjoy ...'

'Enough of that, Thyssen. Get aft! And when we stand down you're going to come back in here and clean that shit off the deck with your bare hands!'

Up on the bridge, Bergman took a last look at the unidentified float-plane. For some reason it seemed oblivious to the alien presence of the U-boat on the surface and was still holding a steady course at a safe distance. Closing the cock of the voice pipe with unhurried care, he swung his legs down into the opened hatch to follow the others below. His body twisted round as his feet touched the rungs of the ladder and reaching up, he shut and clipped the hatch cover.

'Planes to dive - flood tanks!'

Leutnant (Ing.) Badenholdt, U-885's chief engineer, watched the warning lights of the flooding table with an eagle eye. Green for empty like rows of one-eyed traffic signals standing at go.

'Flood!'

His repetition of Bergman's command was the executive order to open the main vents and let the sea into the empty ballast tanks. Keeping his eyes on the serried ranks of green glow-worms hooded Ready to dive on the control panel, he triggered the carefully rehearsed diving routine into action.

'Flood Five; Four; Three; Two; Both!'

Anonymous naked arms reached up towards the steel arch of the control room roof while groping hands located the overhead valve wheels which would open the main vents and release the Kingston valves. Despite the sudden shock of the diving-alarm which had inflamed raw nerve ends and sent pulses racing, each man carried out his allotted task with smooth practised efficiency. Danger had reawakened their sense of discipline and turned them into mindless automatons, no longer thinking men but blindly obedient machines. And intent on their task, the first gut-churning panic quickly subsided. Even Willi Hartmann's mind was on his job for once as he spun down the brass hand-wheel controlling No. 3 tank.

'Five!'

'Four!'

Each man called off his number as the wheel ground against the safety stop that showed it fully open.

'Three!'

'Two!'

'Both!'

The main vents swung open and *U-885* blew gushing geysers of spray from her ballast tanks as she started to submerge. She sank quickly as the sea roared into the empty tanks and only No. 1, the aft tank, was left empty. It was standard diving routine. Flooded forward, the U-boat took on a nose-heavy attitude that drove the bows down at a sharper angle so that she dived more quickly.

'One!' Badenholdt shouted as a solitary green light glowed against a field of red.

Manhaussen, the Obergefreiter stationed under the valve wheel of the stern tank, obeyed immediately. Reaching upwards, he grasped the rim of the wheel with both hands and spun it down. The steepness of the dive eased as the stern grew heavier and Badenholdt checked his panel. The last green light had gone out. It was glowing red across the board.

'All diving tanks flooded, sir!'

Seated at the periscope in the conning-tower command room situated directly above the main control room, Bergman acknowledged the report and pushed his face against the eyepiece of the 'scope. The large sky-search lens tilted upwards and, picking up the last estimated bearing of the mysterious float-plane, he scanned the sky with infinite care.

The black dot was larger now and it was obvious that the bubbling white froth which U-885 had left on the surface when she dived had attracted the pilot's attention.

'Twenty feet, sir.'

Schroeder, standing at his diving position between the two depth-gauges, made his report through the voice pipe as the long red needles fingered past the 20 calibration mark on the white-faced dial.

'Trim at thirty,' Bergman instructed and the Executive Officer passed the order back to the two planesmen sitting at the hydroplane controls.

Von Schroeder frowned with surprise at the skipper's order. Thirty feet was not deep enough to escape either bombs or depth charges. Yet according to the charts, they had plenty of diving depth under the keel. Why the hell was the skipper taking a chance when he had ample time to escape?

But Bergman knew what he was doing - U-885's

Metox apparatus had provided him with a significant clue.

Initially he had blamed Schwarze for not maintaining listening watch on his receiving equipment. But a moment's reflection was sufficient to dismiss the thought from his mind. Unlike Bottcher or the other members of the fore-end's mess, the young Berliner was a good sailor. He was not the type to slacken off just because things were quiet.

Bergman had made good use of *U-885*'s long and uneventful voyage to observe his crew both at work and off-duty. It was a routine part of his technique. And by now he knew which men could be trusted to carry out a task without supervision and which would skimp a job when no one was watching them. He knew, too, who were the steady family men; who were the ambitious ones; and who were fractious. That was one of the reasons he had pounced on Bottcher and why he had given Manhaussen his precious solitary stripe.

Like an omnipotent god in his own little undersea world, he was aware of which men swore. Whether they read and what they read. He even knew which members of the crew dreamed and although he did not know what they dreamed about, in Hartmann's case, he could make a fair guess.

But, and this was the unknown yet vital factor, he had yet to discover by hard experience which had the strongest nerves to withstand the strains of prolonged depth-charging or the courage to remain on deck serving the guns under fire. Such knowledge would only come when *U-885* finally saw action. And he had learned long ago that it proved often the most unlikeliest member of the crew who was most reliable in an emergency.

Outward discipline and steadiness were well and good under normal conditions but they often crumpled under stress.

Even so, and despite these reservations, Bergman instinctively felt he could rely on Schwarze. And it was this subconscious acceptance of the young Berliner's reliability that had given him the clue. If Schwarze had not reported receiving signals from his Fu.M.B. equipment, there could only be one reason - there was no radar pulse to detect.

And if the aircraft was not using radar, it could only be Japanese.

Bergman peered through the eyepiece again as the float plane droned closer. His mouth felt dry and the palms of his hands were damp with sweat. If he was wrong, U-885 stood little chance of escaping now. Evidence and experience warned him to dive deep and escape danger. Yet some intangible and inexplicable hunch urged him to ignore the warning signs and see what happened.

In his earlier career, Bergman had never taken chances. Survival was all that mattered and as soon as danger threatened, he had always taken UB-44 to safety without hesitation. But now, his judgement jaded by constant dangers, with the edge of his awareness blunted by continual conflict with the enemy, he was becoming overconfident in his ability to survive no matter what happened. It was a dangerous state of mind for a submarine commander to have and Bergman knew it. But like the other nagging danger signals, he chose to ignore it.

One by one, he ticked off the identification features of the float-plane as it closed on the U-boat. And then suddenly, as if to demonstrate his infallibility, the Type-

93 seaplane swung through 90° to display the blazing red circles of its national markings daubed under each wing.

'Fire two green - one red!'

Lauerbach, U-885's senior signaller, fed the appropriate cartridges into the ejector, pulled down the lever to seal the breech, and squeezed the trigger. The mechanism coughed obediently and the coloured signal lights hissed from the mouth of the ejector tube alongside the stalk of the periscope. The FK-I9 (Mk III) submerged signalling apparatus had been designed for precisely this situation so that a U-boat travelling below the surface at periscope depth could fire a recognition signal without exposing itself to danger. And by remaining trimmed at thirty feet, Bergman had left himself free to use it.

Watching through the sky-search lens, he saw the three cartridges rise to 200 feet, describe a flat parabola at the zenith of their trajectory like clay pigeons flashing past a marksman in the firing pits, and then sparkle to life.

Green... green... red.

If he'd guessed wrong, taken one chance too many, U-885 would have to dive deep in a desperate race to escape the depth charges cascading from the sky. If he was right, the aircraft would signal an acknowledgement.

Every man in the crew knew that an aircraft was overhead and each was uncomfortably aware that Bergman had drawn attention to their presence with the signal flares. White-faced and tense, lower lips drawn tight against their teeth, they exchanged anxious glances and stared up at the steel roof of their underwater prison as they waited.

Bergman could have told them that the float-plane had answered their recognition signal correctly. But he chose to remain silent. There was nothing like the fear of attack to bring out the best in a crew - or the worst. It was tough on *U-885*'s crew but knowledge of their reaction might prove invaluable in different circumstances.

'Stand by to surface.'

No one spoke but the tension suddenly lifted. And although not a single expression altered, their relief was obvious. Schroeder put the order into execution.

'Stand by to surface. Close main vents. Planes hard a-rise. Blow all tanks.'

'Blowfive! Four! Three! Two! Both!'

Crouched over his diving controls like an ancient alchemist concocting a magical brew, Badenholdt waited for the telltale lights to change from red back to green.

U-885's bows lifted sharply as Oberbootsmann Kosch operated the large diameter wheel controlling the forward hydroplanes. Glancing upwards, he saw the horizontal bar of the inclinometer tilt in a mirrored reflection of the U-boat's nose-up attitude. The doors of the main vents clanged shut in a series of muffled thuds of steel against steel while the interior of the compressed submarine was filled with the high-pitched scream of air as the valves opened to blow the tanks clear of water.

'Blow one! '

The stern tank was the last to be emptied and as Manhaussen screwed the small hand-wheel of the compressed air valve anti clockwise *U-885*'s tail-heavy angle of rise gradually levelled out.

Fifteen... ten... five...

Bergman watched the repeater depth-gauge in the conning-tower room as Kosch intoned the readings from the master indicator in front of his diving station at the bow hydroplane control. The conning tower was now well clear of the surface and *U-885* streamed water from

her drain holes as she emerged from the depths in a cauldron of boiling froth like a sleek grey whale rising from
some gigantic and improbable bubble bath.

'Main engines!'

'Switches off. Clutches in. Start main engines.'

Huddled over his control panel in the motor room,
Machinenmaat Venne reached forward and jerked the
heavy double-poled lever that cut out the motors and the
lamps flickered momentarily as the circuits changed.
Inside the next compartment, his friend Dietrich waited
quietly for Badenholdt's confirmation.

'Open high induction valve.'

Dietrich gripped the steel-handled lever and pulled it
down. Out of sight and high above his head, the flapped
valve of the exhaust intake opened.

'Induction valve open, sir. All secure.'

'Clutches in... start main engines.'

'Slow ahead.'

'Slow ahead, sir.'

The heavy clutch engaged and Obermachinist
Aachan jabbed the green starting button with his thumb.
The diesels responded instantly and bellowed into a full-
throated roar as Aachan revved hard to clear the exhaust
valve of water. Then the throttles eased back, the roar
faded to a gentle rumble, and the twin MAN units
puttered softly at slow speed with a docility that belied
the massive 5,400 horsepower of which they were
capable.

Bergman was in no hurry. What the hell did it
matter? They'd already spent nearly six weeks getting this
far so why rush now? It was too bloody hot anyway. He
scratched his stomach and suppressed a yawn. The sticky
heat had given him an irritating rash which the salt spray

had inflamed into raw angry weals. And he was not the only one. Practically every man in the crew was suffering from skin disorders resulting from the humid heat inside the U-boat and Hoyt, the Sanitasobermaat, had run out of talc over a week earlier. What they needed more than anything else in the world was a shower to wash the sweat and grime from their itching flesh.

The float-plane dipped its wings overhead, circled twice, and turned eastwards towards the still invisible coastline of Penang Island. Bergman watched the aircraft hightailing for the horizon and thought of the hot soothing bath that was waiting.

'Full ahead both! Conning-tower party to the bridge. Diving Watch to stand down.'

Hoisting himself off the saddle seat, he felt the sweat-soaked crotch of his trousers sticking to his flesh and, almost without thinking, he reached down and started scratching again. If he hadn't been celibate for the last six weeks, he'd have sworn he had crabs.

The upper hatch swung open and he clambered out onto U-885's narrow bridge followed by the four duty lookouts. A few moments later, von Schroeder's head emerged into the strong sunlight and with a heave of his powerful shoulders, the Executive Officer lifted himself clear of the hatch and joined the skipper.

'So far, so good, sir.'

Bergman shrugged. 'We've been lucky. But it won't stay like this much longer. Once we clear Penang, we'll be heading straight into the war zone.'

'I suppose you'll grant shore leave, sir.'

'Not if I can avoid it.' Bergman's mouth twisted. 'The men need more training drills before we start for Singapore and I want to spend a couple of days putting them through it. If we let 'em ashore, they'll go wild after being cooped up in this bloody oven for six weeks.'

'Can't say I'd blame them.' von Schroeder grinned. 'I fancy a bit of the old oriental mystery myself. *Zwar von hinten und von vorne.* And if the rumours are true, sideways as well - it's all the same to me.'

Although he heard Hartmann snigger in the background, von Schroeder could sense that Bergman was not amused.

'The men will only be allowed on shore under supervision,' Bergman said crisply. 'You are presumably aware of my views on such things. When I commanded *UB-44*, even the official brothels were placed out of bounds to the men. And the officers,' he added pointedly. 'So unless Japanese etiquette makes refusal impossible, there will be no fraternization with the native women ashore.'

Bloody hypocrite, von Schroeder grumbled to himself. In common with most of the men who had served in the 10th Flotilla, he'd heard all about Bergman's fancy woman in Lorient - and some of the ugly rumours of what had happened to her when the Kapitanleutnant tired of her charms. That was the trouble with these puritans. Have a good time yourself but make sure nobody else gets the chance.

Brecht and Hartmann, standing to port and starboard in the aft lookout stations, exchanged glances at the thought of the forbidden fleshpots. Like von Schroeder, they too relished the ideas of a little Oriental mystery. But if Bergman had his way, any chance of a night ashore would be knocked firmly on the head.

Perhaps Bottcher would have some ideas. He was still shaken up by his recent escape from summary execution. But like the rest of the men in the fore-end's mess, he was beginning to realise that Bergman had never intended to have him shot in the first place so Bottcher had a score to settle with the skipper. And with his long experience of Kriegsmarine routine, Hartmann felt sure that his messmate would be able to evolve some sort of plan to circumvent Bergman's no fraternization order.

'Pay attention, Hartmann! If I see you daydreaming, again you'll be on a charge.'

The lookout stiffened obediently and swung his glasses across his allotted quadrant of the horizon. Why the hell did they have to conscript him into U-boats, he asked himself for the hundredth time. He'd been doing a useful bit of war-work in Hamburg operating his amusement arcade for the entertainment of servicemen on leave. Perhaps if he'd paid off the local Gauleiter after that incident with Gretchen, he wouldn't be where he was right now. But how the hell could he have known she'd got the clap?

And if he had to serve in U-boats, why did it have to be under a bastard like Kapitanleutnant Bergman?

THREE

Commander Fujita's office was a low white-walled villa standing in a cool glade of trees at the end of a steeply-winding path leading up from the harbour. The air was heavy with the scent of jasmine and bougainvillea but the sickly-sweet smell made a refreshing change from the stink of diesel oil diced with stale cabbage and human sweat with which Bergman had lived for the previous six weeks.

The villa itself was invitingly cool and two large ceiling fans stirred the warmly turgid air into a gentle breeze.

'Welcome to Penang, Herr Kapitanleutnant.' Fujita rose up from behind his desk and bowed politely as Bergman was shown into the room. 'You have no doubt had a hard trip and it will be my honour to make your stay a pleasant one.' His hand waved towards a low table set to one side of the desk. 'Tea?' He smiled deprecatingly to reveal his white overlarge teeth. 'Or perhaps you would prefer coffee?'

'Nothing harder?' *U-885* was 'dry' and Bergman had

been looking forward to his first drink almost as much as his first bath.

Fujita walked across to an ornate chromium-fronted cabinet and pulled it open to reveal an Aladdin's cave of liquor that would have triggered an instant riot had *U-885*'s crew seen it.

'Help yourself, Kapitanleutnant. Scotch, gin, brandy - perhaps you prefer American bourbon.' He paused as Bergman reached for a bottle of dimple Haig, pulled off the wire seal, and poured himself a generous measure. 'Iced water over there if you need it.'

Bergman needed it. And a stream of bubbles floated upwards inside the glass reservoir as he held the tumbler under the tap. He swallowed deep, savoured the bite of good Scotch whisky in his stomach, and then sipped soberly.

'I see you have all the comforts of home, Commander,' he observed drily.

Fujita nodded gleefully like a child delighted with his birthday presents. 'Just the spoils of victory,' he chuckled. 'Far better than home I can assure you. This was the American Club before the enemy pulled out of Penang - that's the reason for the air conditioning and iced water dispenser. The Navy was lucky this time. The army had first choice but they preferred the British yacht club building down by the harbour because they liked the look of the Malayan waitresses. But there's no comparison. Plenty of drinks, of course, but it's as stuffy as hell and the walls are covered with stuffed animal heads and cricket photographs. And,' he chuckled again, 'the waitresses all ran away after the first night.'

Bergman poured himself another drink. Fujita joined him at the cabinet and, selecting a small bourbon, he raised his glass. 'To friendship, Kapitanleutnant.'

Bergman clinked glasses with him. He had anticipated the usual stiffly-formal routine of Oriental politenesses and he appreciated the Commander's direct approach. But he took care to emphasise his own position as guest.

'To the Emperor and our alliance.'

Fujita accepted the toast, swallowed his bourbon in a single gulp, and put the empty glass back on top of the cocktail cabinet.

'As it is necessary for us to speak in the language of our enemy, it seems foolish to retain the formalities of rank, Kapitanleutnant. My name is Mitsuru.'

'Konrad.' Bergman held out his hand and they exchanged grasps with a warmth that had been missing from their first greeting. 'Tell me, Mitsuru, are all Japanese like you?'

'Regrettably, no,' Fujita admitted sadly. 'You see, I spent several years in the United States before the war.' He grinned slyly. I'm afraid I picked up a few of their more degenerate ways. Most officers of the Imperial Navy are very formal and rank counts for everything. You must bear that in mind, my friend, when you get to Tokyo.'

'Thanks for the tip. Now before we get down to business regarding the facilities for the proposed U-boat base, can I ask a favour?'

'Of course.'

'Is there anywhere in this Godforsaken hole I can get a bath?'

Fujita nodded. 'Forgive me for not offering it to you when you arrived but I thought you'd prefer a drink first. Unfortunately, the British blew up the pumping station before they left and there's no piped water supply. But if you are willing to make do with a traditional Japanese bath, it can be arranged.' Bergman didn't know what a traditional bath involved but he didn't want to show his ignorance of Japanese customs. He nodded. 'That will be fine. Believe me, after six weeks in that stinking boat, I wouldn't care if someone just threw buckets of cold water over me.'

Fujita smiled inscrutably and there was an unexpected gleam of amusement in his black eyes.

'There is an officer's bathing area just behind the clubhouse at the top of the hill,' he explained. 'Would you like me to arrange similar facilities for your men?'

'Later will do. Right now, they're off on a route march to take the edge off their appetites and give them a bit of exercise. I'll let you know this evening and perhaps we can arrange something then.'

The small clearing at the rear of the villa was completely empty except for a number of buckets and a large water tank. Bergman could see no sign of a bath anywhere and no huts or screens for undressing. Except for two Japanese sailors sitting on the ground in the shade of the tall bushes that ran along one side of the clearing, the area seemed deserted.

Fujita, seemingly unconcerned by the lack of privacy, began unfastening the buttons of his uniform while Bergman hesitated irresolutely. The shirt came off and as he threw it down on the grass, the two sailors stood up and started to fill the buckets from the large galvanised iron tank. They showed a similar lack of concern at Fujita's impromptu striptease and their faces were completely impassive as they trotted backwards and forwards with the buckets.

When he was down to his cotton underpants, Fujita glanced up at Bergman. The Kapitanleutnant was still fully dressed.

'Don't look so shocked, Konrad. This is the traditional Japanese bath. And if you don't strip off and join me, you won't get another until that pumping station's repaired.'

Fujita's discarded pants joined the rest of his clothing on the grass and he paddled over to the improvised shower. His nut-brown body was tightly muscular and he was totally unselfconscious about his nakedness. One of the sailors handed him a bucket and without more ado, Fujita lifted it high above his head and tilted the water over himself.

'It's great!' he shouted to Bergman. The water streaming down his face plastered his black hair over his forehead like greased tails. 'Come on - don't be shy. Back home in Kyoto we have mixed bathing so I don't know what you're worried about.'

On an impulse, Bergman threw discretion to the wind. What the hell - when in Rome and all that. And Fujita certainly looked invitingly cool as he tipped a second bucket over himself. Bergman ripped open his shirt, shrugged it over his head, and unfastened his belt. A few moments later, he was standing next to the little Japanese officer and taking a bucket from one of the sailors.

The cool water sluicing down his sweating body felt like ice although, as Bergman well knew, it was only tepid. It splattered around his feet like one of the mountain streams in his beloved Bavaria and he could feel the water trickling sensuously over his skin. He grunted his thanks as he was handed another bucket and, taking a deep breath, he raised his arms high above his head and repeated the operation.

The primitive ritual reminded him of his schooldays, standing naked under the showers with a dozen other boys after a hectic game of football. The cool refreshing water seemed to wash the years of stress and strain away, taking him back to the carefree days before the war.

Fujita took another bucket but instead of turning it over himself, he balanced it carefully, took aim, and sloshed it over his companion.

Bergman jerked with the sudden unexpected shock but he saw the joke and grabbing a bucket, he retaliated promptly. It was like a snowball fight only they were using buckets of water instead of snow. And after weeks of being cooped up in the hot confines of U-885's iron hull, it was an exhilarating experience. Even the two sailors were grinning as they ran up with fresh ammunition for the two contestants and at that glorious moment, Bergman felt as if nothing else existed in the world except the joy of dousing his companion with a bucket of water before receiving the contents of Fujita's reply full in the face.

He was too engrossed in his private game to hear the steady tramp of marching boots climbing the path to the American Club. And Leutnant Teschen was unfortunately unaware that his skipper was standing stark naked just beyond the bushes.

The route march which Bergman had ordered had not been welcomed by U-885's crew - their idea of exercise took a different form and involved another set of muscles altogether - and they grumbled glumly as Teschen led them up the steep gravel path towards the clearing at the top of the hill.

Kosch had attempted to raise their spirits by singing the *Horst Wessel* but the words had rapidly degenerated into a bawdy barrack-room version and for the last half mile the men had marched in resentful silence.

'Trying to wear us out so we'll be too tired to fancy it,' Bottcher said out of the comer of his mouth to no one in particular.

'That'll be the day,' Hartmann grinned. 'And why worry - out East the men just lie back and enjoy it. They tell me these Oriental tarts prefer doing all the hard work. 'Ain't that right, Erich?'

'Quiet in the ranks,' Manhaussen told him sharply. 'You're in enough trouble already so don't make it worse.'

'*Grossen Schwanz,*' Hartmann spat. But he did as he was ordered despite his truculence.

The straggly column, hardly a credit to the *Kriegsmarine* in their soiled white shorts and sweaty vests, toiled up the hill only too happy to accept the reprimand and save their breath for the steep climb to the summit. A route march wasn't their idea of shore leave and even Schwarze found himself cursing the skipper as he trudged on.

The path curved sharply to the right when it reached the top of the hill and the column obediently followed Leutnant Teschen. Then suddenly they were through the screen of bushes and into the clearing.

'Eyes left!'

Teschen had not given the command. The voice, familiar yet unidentifiable, had come from the rear ranks of the column. And as he turned to bawl out the culprit, he saw Bergman and Commander Fujita standing stark naked in the centre of the arid patch of grass.

'Eyes front!'

But it was too late. Hartmann sniggered and the dam burst. Unknown lips pursed in lewd whistles and there were jeering laughs from the rear ranks. Then suddenly the men fell silent and marched stolidly on as if nothing untoward had happened.

Bergman could not even grab a towel. The column had appeared from nowhere without warning and, caught literally with his pants down, there was no time to cover himself. But uncomfortably aware of Fujita's astonishment at the behaviour of the U-boat men and disregarding his own embarrassment, he turned his head in the direction of the departing column. Personal feelings no longer entered into it - the honour of the Navy was at stake.

'*A*-bout... TURN!'

The unexpected command brought the men about with the precision of a parade-ground demonstration. It never occurred to anyone to ignore the order on the premise that it was not intended for them; there was something in Bergman's voice that betokened instant obedience.

'Column – *halt!*'

Bergman noted with satisfaction that not a single man moved as they stamped to a halt. They knew they were in for something.

'Column - right *turn!*'

Crun-n-ch.. .crunch.

'Officers and NCOs fall out.'

Still naked, his legs slightly apart and his hands resting on his hips, Bergman slowly surveyed the line of men, pausing long enough to search the face of each man in turn. Standing like carved stone statues, they met his eyes unflinchingly.

'Strip off!'

The mouths of the U-boatmen gaped in disbelief. It must be a joke. He wouldn't dare to humiliate them in public like this.

'That's an order.'

My God, thought Teschen, he means it. The men would never forget this. Hearing soft giggles behind his back, the young Leutnant turned his head and saw a group of Malayan women peering from the bushes and pointing at the sailors as they removed their clothes.

Bergman took his trousers from one of the Japanese sailors and pulled them on casually. Fujita, too, was getting dressed. He stood to one side watching curiously. In the Imperial Japanese Navy, such behaviour towards an officer would have resulted in each man being punched in the face by a petty officer. Yet, in many ways, Bergman's form of punishment was the more brutal. Physical pain quickly passed. But the mental anguish of indignity and public humiliation could scar a man's self-respect for life. And having spent three months in charge of the women's prison camp at Selimpore, he knew about such things.

'Running on the spot. Be-*gin!*'

Bergman's mouth was tight as he watched the two ranks of men jogging up and down in the hot sun, their arms straight and rigid at their sides, their faces flushed with embarrassment and exertion.

'Knees up! Come on - *up – up*' He turned to Teschen. 'Take over, Herr Leutnant. And keep them at it for five minutes. After that, get them back on board *U-885* at the double!'

'Sir.'

Leaving the young officer to take charge of the

punishment squad, Bergman took Fujita's arm and guided him back towards the commandeered American club. The group of native women who had gathered to watch the antics of the German sailors was growing larger every moment as news of the unexpected display of masculine talent spread through the town and the two officers had to force their way through the excited throng.

Bergman had already decided that there would be no more shore leave for the men for the rest of their stay in Penang. And it appealed to his odd sense of humour to let the women see what they were missing...

Fujita poured another drink, carried it across the room, and rejoined Bergman by the opened window looking down over Swettenham pier and the calm-watered expanse of Penang Harbour.

'It can be a mistake to be too hard with your men,' he observed casually as he settled into the cane chair. 'I have always found that it leads to resentment.'

Bergman was mellowing under the influence of the liquor. Dusk had fallen and the cool evening air had soothed his temper. He shrugged. 'Perhaps you're right, Mitsuru. But they're an undisciplined bunch of bloody pirates and they've been asking for something like this for a long time.'

Fujita sipped his drink slowly. 'No doubt they have, Konrad. But you've demonstrated your authority. If I were in your place, I'd say it was time to hold out the olive branch.'

'I thought the Japanese Navy had the toughest discipline in the world,' Bergman objected. 'Your people seem none the worse for it.'

'Perhaps so - but, as I told you, I have spent many years in the west. The type of man who serves in your U-boats is not like the ignorant peasants we enlist as sailors. They've had their punishment and they'll accept it - providing you show them you're human.'

Bergman knew Fujita was talking sense but the arrogance of command made him reluctant to admit his error. He had been a martinet throughout the long and gruelling voyage from Lorient to Malaya and he was aware that, as he grew older, he had more inclination to hold himself apart from his crew. The men of *UB-44* had known him as a man as well as their commanding officer with the result that they had accepted his perfectionism without resentment. But the crew of *U-885* had seen little of him. They knew only of his reputation and they were frightened of him. Perhaps Fujita was right in his analysis - the onlooker often sees more of the game than the players.

'And how do I show them that?' he asked defiantly.

'Give them some proper shore leave for a start. Let them work off their high spirits and get it out of their system.'

Bergman sighed. 'You obviously don't know my crew. Half of the men are the dregs of the Kriegsmarine. I think they only sent them out with me because they think we'll never get back to Germany again. I wouldn't dare let them loose in Penang - they'd wreck the town inside an hour.'

'Then why not send them along to one of our official establishments? I'll arrange for the shore patrols to keep an eye on them. And if they smash up Navy property, it won't matter too much.'

'What establishment?' Bergman asked.

'I suppose you'd call it a military brothel?' Fujita spread his hands deprecatingly. 'I don't approve but it means that the men can enjoy themselves without risk and under supervision.' Bergman didn't like the idea either but he had sense enough to understand the point Fujita was making. And there was no doubt that *U-885*'s men would appreciate the gesture.

'Very well,' he agreed with sudden decision. 'I will allow the off-duty Watch six hours leave. The others can come ashore tomorrow evening.'

Fujita mixed Bergman another drink and placed it on the low bamboo table alongside his chair.

'Naturally, you must have your relaxations, too,' he said confidentially. 'Although, of course, I would not expect you to share the same facilities as your men.'

'I'm too bloody tired for that sort of thing,' Bergman parried quickly. 'In any case, I have several hours paper-work when I get back on board tonight. Doenitz will want a full report on my recommendations concerning the flotilla base at Penang.'

'But I insist, Konrad.' Fujita gripped his arm and leaned closer. 'The Navy officers have brought a couple of *geishas* down from Tokyo - really high-lass girls. It's just what you need.'

Bergman realised that his excuses, valid though they were, were being treated as politeness and he knew that the little Japanese Commander would be offended if he refused. It was important to maintain goodwill if the Kreigsmarine wanted to use Penang as a U-boat base and he scratched his ear as he searched for a way out of the situation.

'I appreciate your invitation, Mitsuru,' he said slowly. 'In fact, I agree it would probably do me good. But perhaps tomorrow night - it's been a hard day. We must have spent all of three hours tramping around the harbour inspecting the facilities.'

'Nonsense, Konrad, you're as tough as a bull. A

couple of hours rest and you'll be fit for anything a woman can offer.' His overlarge teeth gleamed as he smiled. 'And I'll make sure you have the services of Yokoshi - she's the best of the two.' Bergman knew sufficient of Japanese culture to appreciate that a *geisha* was not a prostitute in the Western sense of the word. She was a girl trained from the earliest age to amuse and entertain men. She might indeed sleep with a patron but, if she did, it was entirely of her own free will and by her own choice. The fee paid only for her other services - not her body.

Perhaps he could get away with it. Perhaps he could make the girl understand and no doubt, thanks to her training, she would make no physical demands upon him.

'You must come along tonight,' Fujita urged. 'We had a senior official arrive from Tokyo this morning and he especially wanted Yoko - apparently he had been entertained by her before the war. I told him that you had reserved her services this evening and if you don't come along he will think I am deliberately deceiving him.'

Bergman was not particularly interested in either the politics of prostitution or Japanese etiquette. In fact, he was feeling too tired to listen and Fujita's high-pitched sing-song voice was making him feel sleepy. It was easier to give in than resist. At least he would get a few hours rest before he had to accept Fujita's invitation and anything could happen in that time.

'I RECKON the old bastard's not so bad after all.'

Hartmann's normally pallid face was flushed with exertion as he raised himself from the soft sprawled body on the bed. A pair of slanting black eyes glittered up at him.

'You like Chikiki... no?'

Hartmann thrust down hard to keep her quiet.

'I like Chikiki ... yes! But for Christ's sake give me a breather. I've got out of practice since I joined the Navy.' He heaved himself up with his arms and Chikiki pouted as he left her. Swinging his legs over the side of the old-fashioned iron bedstead, Willi looked across the room. Bottcher, despite his bulk, was almost invisible but Hart-mann could just see his fat buttocks bouncing up and down on the bed opposite.

He lit a cigarette and poured himself another glass of canned American beer. For the first time in two months, he felt at peace with the world. Taking a gulp of tepid beer, he nodded at Hugo Brecht who, like himself, was sitting on the edge of the next bed and getting his breath back. He was drinking beer from the can with one hand and stroking the brown-skinned Malayan girl stretched out naked beside him with the other.

'I doubt it,' Brecht said sourly. 'More probably the bastard's scared of what we'd do to him after that exhibi-tion this afternoon. But I don't reckon he's so bad as you make out.'

The girl lying beside him giggled as his fingers gently rolled her dark brown nipple. She reached up, pulled him down by the neck, and began kissing him violently. Brecht pushed her away and returned to his beer.

'We all know you've got it in for the skipper, Willi,' he went on. 'But to be honest, I think the day'll come when we'll be glad we've got someone like him looking after us.'

'Crap! He's a bastard and he always will be.' Hart-mann reached back and pushed Chikiki away. 'And you

can lay off too, you bitch. I need a bloody rest. Go find
some other screw.' Chikiki's dark eyes smouldered resent-
fully. But in her profession, she was hardened to insults.
A girl couldn't work in a Singapore brothel for three years
and retain her dignity. She looked across the room and
beckoned to Dietrich. The sailor didn't need a second
invitation - there were only six girls and that wasn't
enough to go round two dozen hungry U-boatmen. He
put down his beer and hurried across.

She raised her legs to receive the over-eager Dietrich
and one knee banged Hartmann sharply in the small of
his back. He swore, jabbed his elbow into her flexed thigh,
and stood up. There was no room on the bed for three
people.

Having tired of listening to Willi's views on the skipper's character, Brecht rolled over again and, still holding
the half-emptied beer can in his left hand, he was
pumping hard at the spread-eagled body stretched
beneath him. Willi bent forward across the bed, grabbed
his messmate by the shoulder, and dragged him away
from the panting woman.

'Lay off, you randy bastard. You can't have second
helpings while the rest of the lads are still waiting for their
first.' Brecht grumbled bitterly although, secretly, he was
glad of the respite. Mauru was wearing him out but he
didn't dare to cry quits or he'd never have lived it down
with the rest of the men in the fore-ends mess. He stood
up with all the appearance of outraged reluctance
although a casual glance was sufficient to show that he
was by no means as physically eager as he pretended.

Sept Garnheim raced to take his place on the bed and
Brecht heard Mauru's simulated groan of pleasure as U-
885's second radio operator drove into her.

The converted barrack room was sparsely furnished and sordid. A makeshift bar consisting of wooden boards balanced precariously on empty beer crates took up the far end of the hut and extended its tentacles down the long wall. Three ramshackle iron beds occupied the opposite wall with another three facing almost diagonally opposite. There were no partitions or privacy and the men writhing on the beds were urged on by the jeers and obscene comments of their partnerless comrades sitting at the bar. There was no room for modesty or inhibitions and the cramped smoke-filled hut was thick with the smell of sex and hard liquor.

Brecht grabbed a tumbler of Johnnie Walker Black Label from the Malayan bartender and swallowed a mouthful.

'Like I said, Willi. You've got the skipper all wrong. I know he's a tough bastard to serve under but most times we get all we ask for. I used to know a torpedoman on *UB-44* and he said Bergman was the best skipper in the U-boat service.'

'And what happened to him?' Hartmann asked sourly.

'He was lost when *UB-44* went down last year but you can't blame that on Bergman.'

'I can,' Hartmann said pointedly. 'Strange he was the only officer to get away when the boat went down,' he added.

'Nothing strange about it at all.' Brecht had started on his second double Scotch and the unfamiliar liquor was making him belligerent. 'I can think of lots of cases where the captain has been the only survivor from a submarine. What are you getting at, Willi?'

Hartmann patted his nose meaningfully with a

yellow-stained finger. 'I'm not saying *what* I know, Hugo. But I heard plenty of stories about that episode *and* a few others he was mixed up in. I could tell...'

The sentence was cut short as Bottcher joined them at the bar. A pair of khaki drill shorts hung low under his pot belly and his fleshy body was dripping with sweat. His place on the rumpled bed had already been taken by one of the waiting men and Chien-lu - lithe, small-boned, and tiny-breasted - was devouring her new lover with the passionate ferocity of a tiger to the catcalls and whistles of the eager onlookers.

Max Bottcher, eighteen stone of fat and muscle and a stevedore at Bremen's commercial docks before he'd enlisted in 1937, had selected the tiny olive-skinned girl because he relished the thought of her begging for mercy. But she had given him as good as he gave and, red-faced and perspiring, he was only too glad to obtain quick satisfaction before handing her over to someone else.

'I was saying to Willi that the skipper's not such a bad guy after all, Max. He's certainly doing us proud tonight.'

Bottcher grabbed a bottle from the bartender, put it to his mouth, and sucked the rum down into his belly. Then, belching loudly, he put it back on the counter and finished buttoning his flies.

'Sure, tonight he's doing us all right. But tomorrow he'll be sweating our guts on some lousy drill and bawling us out when we're too tired to work.' Bottcher hadn't forgiven the mental agony of his mock execution the day before. 'If you ask me, he's just letting us run ourselves into the ground so that he has an excuse to step up the punishment rota tomorrow. Sadistic bastard.'

'Wonder where he is now?' Brecht mused. The

Scotch whisky had burned his guts and he was treating it with more caution this time.

'Probably sitting in his cabin reading OKM regulations so he can trip us up over something new.'

Hartmann shook his head knowingly. 'No, he isn't. I was talking to Manhaussen earlier on and he told me the Old Man had been invited up to the Japanese Officer's Club this evening for a free poke at their *geisha* girls.'

Bottcher let out a sneering laugh. 'Bergman in bed with a *geisha* - you must be joking. He wouldn't even know which bloody end to start...'

'Does it matter with a *geisha*?'

Rat-tat-tat-tat-tat-tat-tat!

'What the hell was that?' Brecht sobered and looked up. He put his glass down on the bar and listened. The other men had heard the sound as well and the noise inside the brothel suddenly hushed. Even those on the beds raised themselves up breathlessly from the sweating women sprawled wide-legged beneath them and tried to concentrate their thoughts. *Rat-tat-tat-tat... rat-tat-tat-tat-tat!*

'Machine guns!' For all his sloth, Bottcher had seen enough combat service to recognise the familiar chatter. 'Come on, lads - outside!'

'Think the British are launching a counterattack?' Brecht asked no one in particular as they pushed out through the door.

'Not a chance,' someone replied. 'More likely a commando raid of some sort.'

It was pitch dark outside the hut and Bottcher called the men together before they became scattered and lost in the tropical blackness. So far as he could see, the entire leave-party was present. Even the six men disturbed at their labours of love a few moments earlier had joined the group and they were still struggling to pull on their pants as Bottcher shouted them into line.

Obergefrieter Manhaussen had been dozing peacefully in a parked truck outside the hut when the machine-gun fire tore the air. A devout Lutheran, he was not interested in the fleshpots of Penang and having delivered the liberty men to the brothel, he chose to wait in the vehicle until they had finished.

Drawing his service-issue Luger from its holster, he joined the others in the darkness and took command of the situation.

'Spread out, lads. The shooting seems to come from the direction of the Officer's Club. Let's see what's going on.'

'What is it?' Bottcher demanded. 'A raid?'

'No idea - I haven't seen any more than you have. But the Kapitanleutnant is probably up at the club so let's get moving - *raus, raus.*'

A few hundred yards from the white-walled villa, a Japanese sentry swung around nervously and raised his rifle. It was fortunate that Manhaussen was wearing his uniform - the rest of *U-885*'s crew looked like a mob of Chinese pirates. The sentry blinked myopically.

'Where's the shooting - what's going on?' Manhaussen demanded.

The soldier's eyes flickered nervously from left to right as more and more half-naked pale-skinned men appeared out of the darkness. Raising the gun higher, he jabbered something in a sing-song voice.

'Stupid bastard can't speak German,' Hartmann said. 'He doesn't understand a bloody word you're saying,' he told Manhaussen.

Bottcher settled the impasse in characteristic fashion. Throwing himself forward, he wrenched the rifle from the guard's hands and shouldered him to the ground.

'*Kleine votze!*' he spat. He threw the gun to Hartmann. 'Here, Willi - you take it. You're more useful with a rifle than the rest of us.'

Moving cautiously forward and keeping under cover of the hibiscus bushes skirting the boundaries of the villa, the sailors worked their way to the rear of the building. The Club was in darkness but they could hear faint movements inside as the occupants searched for cover in case the machine gun opened up again.

Manhaussen stopped as he reached the corner of the villa. He called up the rest of the party and pointed towards a small building standing at the end of the croquet lawn behind the Club.

'Over there - look! '

The windows of the summerhouse were shattered and the plaited bamboo door swung brokenly on its hinges. The building was in complete darkness but the keen eyes of the U-boatmen, trained for night vision, could see a shadowy figure emerging from the doorway with a submachine gun crooked under its arm.

'Halt!'

As the figure turned in the direction of Manhaussen's shouted command, Bottcher led the others across the clipped grass lawn in a wild charge. The machine gun swung up and flame spurted from the ejector slot. Two of the sailors stumbled and fell as a curtain of bullets hosed into the charging mob and Hartmann threw himself flat on the damp grass. Bottcher and Brecht hit the ground simultaneously and lay face down, waiting for the opportunity to hurl themselves forward again as soon as the machine gun's ammunition clip was exhausted.

'Get him, Willi! *Get him!'*

Hartmann did not need Bottcher's encouragement. The brass face of the rifle butt nestled into his shoulder, his left elbow braced awkwardly under the line of the barrel, and he squinted down the sight.

Crack!

The bullet ricocheted in a wailing shriek after chipping a lump of plaster from the wall twelve inches above the machine-gunner's head.

'Auswurf!'

Willi swore and edged the barrel down a fraction. The sights were set too high. He aimed lower to correct the error.

Crack!

The mysterious machine-gunner was thrown back by the impact of the bullet and his weapon fell to the ground with a clatter. Hartmann wetted his thin lips with the tip of his tongue, tore back the bolt, and fired again.

Crack!.

The man fell forward onto his face with his arms sprawled awkwardly on the wet grass. His legs jerked twice in a rictus of pain and then suddenly he was still.

Bottcher was on his feet at the same instant and with Brecht close behind, he ran towards the summerhouse. No one really knew what they expected to find inside but their blood was up and the hunt demanded another kill. Manhaussen reached the splintered door first and he gestured Bottcher to stand back. Then, holding his pistol ready, he kicked the remains of the door inwards and cautiously poked his head into the little hut. The other three members of the fore-end's mess were at his heels and Hartmann thrust the rifle forward in case of an ambush.

But inside there was nothing but the stillness of death. Apart from an overturned chair in the entrance lobby, there were no outward signs of violence and Manhaussen led them carefully towards the communicating door. He pulled the handle, swung it open, and then stopped dead in his tracks as if frozen rigid with horror. The gun fell limply to his side and he swayed on his feet. Bottcher pushed the Obergefrieter aside and stepped into the room followed by Hartmann.

'Christ Almighty!'

The delicately-furnished bedroom was a complete shambles. The splintered remains of furniture littered the floor, there were gaping gouges in the plaster walls where bullets had ripped in all directions and in the centre of the room lay the sprawled body of a naked *geisha*, her chest and belly torn by heavy calibre bullets at close-range. Bright red blood had sprayed the walls and trickled down to form spreading pools on the floor and Brecht's knees suddenly gave way as he took in the scene. Turning to one side, he was violently sick where he stood.

It was Willi Hartmann who spotted the trail of blood leading behind the bamboo screen and, stepping carefully over the butchered remains of the girl, he dragged the screen down to reveal a rumpled blood-soaked bed.

'It's the Kapitanleutnant!'

The man lying face-down on the bed had three ugly bullet holes punched in his naked back. He was still wearing his blue uniform trousers and crumpled beneath him was a once-white shirt and an officer's jacket.

In the face of death, the bitter resentment faded. It

was Bottcher who first found words adequate to describe their feelings. 'Poor bastard,' he said simply.

'Brecht was right. He wasn't such a bad skipper for all we said about him,' Willi agreed. 'I've known worse.'

Manhaussen was too choked to speak. Pushing the pistol back into its holster, he walked slowly across to the bed and leaned over the dead man. Then placing his hands gently on the naked shoulders, he braced his knees against the edge of the bed and turned the corpse over onto its back.

The head rolled limply to one side and the unseeing eyes stared blankly up at the ceiling while the three men stared down in horror at the brutalised remains of a man who, despite the gold rings on his sleeve, was still a shipmate.

'My God!' Hartmann whispered. 'It's not Bergman - it's Teschen!'

FOUR

For the twentieth time that day, Bergman banged his fist down on Commander Fujita's polished wooden desk top.

'With all due respect, I don't care what you say. Whoever the killer was he didn't want Teschen - he wanted me! Even you were unaware that I'd sent him ashore to take my place.'

Fujita's bland expression gave nothing away. 'But it's ridiculous, Konrad. First, who on earth even knows you are here in Penang. And secondly, why should anyone want to assassinate you?'

Bergman could think of several good reasons but he didn't have time to explain them to the Commander. Yet, considered objectively, he did not see how even the long arm of the Gestapo could reach out as far as Malaya. But what other explanation could there be? Fujita's theory of mistaken identity or some blood feud about the girl, Yoko, was plausible enough but the Kapitanleutnant couldn't bring himself to accept it. 'You say the man was Japanese?' he queried sharply.

Fujita nodded. 'Yes. I mentioned him to you

yesterday afternoon. He had flown in from Tokyo on some special mission. I asked no questions - his papers were in order and countersigned by the C-in-C 5th Fleet.'

'Why not?' Bergman persisted. 'You're supposed to be responsible for security here, aren't you?'

Fujita shrugged disarmingly. 'One does not ask questions of the *Kempei Tai*,' he explained simply.

''*Kempei Tai* - what's that?' Bergman frowned.

'The Japanese secret police. A similar organisation to your Gestapo I believe.'

So his suspicions were right. They were after him. Bergman's expression gave no hint of the thoughts flashing wildly through his mind as he digested Fujita's unintentional bombshell. He'd been a damned fool to think he could escape the clutches of the Gestapo by running away. Obviously, Gorst had tipped off the *Kempei Tai* and they'd wasted no time in trying to square accounts on his behalf.

'I see what you mean, Mitsuru. As you say, one doesn't ask the secret police awkward questions - at least, not if *you* want a quiet life.'

Fujita's dark eyes looked at him shrewdly as if weighing up Bergman's motives and loyalties. Satisfied with what he saw, he leaned forward across the desk.

'I gather you've had trouble with your people as well. So you know what it's like,' he said softly. 'I've spent more than two years trying to get the *Kempei Tai* off my back. Anyone who has spent long periods abroad, especially in America, is immediately suspect. In fact, if it weren't for the protection of my naval uniform, I doubt if I would have lasted this long.'

Although he liked and respected the little Japanese officer, Bergman cautiously avoided a direct answer. Once again, as in Occupied France, he was in a strange land. And once again, he had the same unnerving feeling that every man's hand was against him.

'Let's stop talking about personal matters, Mitsuru. My first task is to get *U-885* away from Penang before there's any further trouble. We can always discuss things later - when the war is over.'

Fujita understood the Kapitanleutnant's reluctance to talk. With typical Japanese fatalism, he did not worry about the future. What would be, would be. If the *Kempei Tai* caught up with him, he would meet his ancestors sooner than he had anticipated. But, aware of the Western way of looking at such things, he could sympathise with Bergman's determination to survive. Death to a German - or an Englishman or an American - was something to be avoided and delayed as long as possible. For a Japanese, it was a welcome release to a better life. He rose out of his chair.

'My men have been loading fresh supplies and water since dawn. I am sorry that we cannot offer you fuel oil as well but we are already short even for our own boats.'

'I have made my own arrangements for bunkering,' Bergman said enigmatically. 'I was warned that Japan was low on oil reserves. And I'm not averse to picking up a tanker and helping myself if the situation becomes critical.' He picked up his uniform cap and held out his hand. 'Well, thanks for everything, Mitsuru. I'm sorry about the trouble last night. I hope you won't get blamed.'

'But there is no need to say goodbye, Konrad.' Fujita had pulled on his own gold-peaked cap and was coming round the side of the desk. 'I shall be sailing to Tokyo with you.'

'The hell you are.'

Fujita's teeth gleamed as he smiled. 'I'm due for a spell of home leave and, of course, you are an officer short on *U-885* since Teschen's death. So I put a call through to my immediate boss, Vice Admiral Nakachi, and he okayed it this morning.'

'But how ...?'

Fujita slid open the drawer of his filing cabinet and gently lifted out a small bronze casket. He held it up for Bergman to see and flicked open the lid. It was filled with a fine grey dust.

'Regretfully, the last earthly remains of our little *geisha*,' he explained sorrowfully. 'I happened to know that Admiral Nakachi was her patron before the war although, naturally, he did not publicise the fact. And so when I offered to bring her ashes back to Japan, he agreed.'

Bergman grinned. It was impossible not to like the irrepressible little Commander. And his deviousness appealed to a similar streak in Bergman's own character. He had a strange premonition that with Fujita's guidance, his mission might be successful after all. It was a gamble, of course, but what decision wasn't in war.

'I hope you know something about submarines,' he observed doubtfully. 'We've no room for passengers, especially with Teschen gone.'

'I spent seven years in the submarine service,' Fujita beamed proudly. 'And I was in command of *I-79* at Pearl Harbor. If it hadn't been for the *Kempei Tai*, I'd be serving in them still. But when they decided that I could not be trusted, they had me posted to a shore appointment.'

'And *are* you to be trusted, Mitsuru?' Bergman asked good-humouredly.

Fujita's impassive face was, if it were possible, even more inscrutable than usual. 'You'll have to find that out for yourself, my dear Kapitanleutnant,' he bowed. 'More importantly, can I trust *you?*'

———

U-885'S BOWS cut the smooth water like a graceful yacht on a carefree pleasure cruise. The sun, standing high in the cloudless noon sky, transformed the bow wave into a cascade of glittering diamonds and only the dull grey war-paint and the ugly snout of the 88mm deck gun marred the peaceful serenity of the scene as the submarine throbbed northwards through a chain of palm-fringed islands.

The Penang incident had exercised a profound influence on the U-boat's normally undisciplined crew and the experience of death close at hand had dampened their usual high spirits. Teschen had been *U-885*'s most popular officer mainly because, young and inexperienced, they could take advantage of him with impunity. But with his death, this fact had been conveniently forgotten and the men were already looking upon him as a hero. And the loss of their two comrades cut down by the assassin's machine-gun fire had added a new and personal dimension to the reality of war.

Bergman's action, too, had surprised them by its total unexpectedness.

On receiving a report of the incident from Obergefrieter Manhaussen, he had called Bottcher, Hartmann and Brecht to his cabin to commend them personally on their initiative and resource. Then, once *U-885* was safely clear of the Singapore danger zone, he had assembled the entire crew on deck and in a simple ceremony awarded Willi Hartmann with the Iron Cross, Second Class for, the decisive part he had played in killing the assassin.

From being the despised weakling of the fore-end's mess, Willi found himself the hero of the moment while Bottcher and Brecht, his most intimate messmates, basked in the reflected glory. The fact that less than a week before any one of the unholy trio would have jumped at an opportunity to push the skipper overboard when no one was looking was conveniently forgotten. The Kapitanleutnant, for all his faults, had shown himself to be human and somewhat to their surprise, the men found they were prepared to do anything he demanded of them.

Bergman showed no surprise at the miraculous change in attitude. The attempt on his life had reawakened the spark of humanity he had so ruthlessly crushed out after Rahel Yousoff's death. And Fujita's advice had made him take stock of himself and realise that a ship with a bad crew usually also had a bad captain.

But, thankfully, the recriminations were now all in the past. True, they weren't as good as the men who had served under him on the old *UB*-44 but there was still time to work them up to the required pitch of efficiency. And at least they were now willing and enthusiastic.

Perhaps the only jarring note during the long passage northeastward, was the presence of the little bronze casket which Fujita insisted on keeping in the wardroom. Bergman had several times tried to persuade his companion to hide it out of sight but Fujita was adamant. And whenever Bergman was off-duty in the wardroom, the casket was a continual reminder of his own narrow escape from the *Kempei Tai*.

Not that he felt any guilt over Teschen's murder. His

only reason for sending the young officer to visit the *geisha* in his place had been no more than sheer physical exhaustion coupled with a curious revulsion towards sex which had dogged him ever since his final meeting with Rahel in the Gestapo's Lorient office the previous year. For once, his conscience was clear and he knew he bore no moral responsibility for the *Kempei Tai's* mistaken identification.

The sun was an enormous ball of fire on the horizon as von Schroeder came through the hatch to take over the Evening Watch. Bergman turned away from the rail, acknowledged the salute, and briefed him for the next Watch.

'We shall be entering the American submarine patrol area sometime in the next twelve hours, Oberleutnant. Make sure the lookouts are on their toes. Fujita tells me the Yanks are doing plenty of damage and they're right on the ball. I hope to get our radar fixed when we reach Japan but until then we've only got our eyes. So don't take any chances.'

'Have the Americans got radar, sir?'

'You bet your life they have - that's why they're running circles around the Nips. But at least we've still got our *Metox* and we might pick up their pulses before they spot us so we've got at least one advantage over the Japs. And I don't intend to have come this far through the war to get sunk by some gum-chewing Yankee cowboy!'

'Any other orders, sir?'

'No, Oberleutnant. But call me an hour before sunrise.'

'Very good, sir. Goodnight, sir.'

Bergman checked the lookouts, enjoyed a last lingering look at the brilliant red sunset on the horizon, and slid down the ladder into the control room. The interior of the U-boat was still unbearably hot but, moving northwards, the temperature was falling slowly and at least they could look forward to some respite from the eternal heat in the near future. He entered the log, signed it, and moved across to the aft watertight bulkhead and the *Metox* receiver.

Schwarze glanced up as Bergman's shadow fell across the apparatus.

'There are Yankee submarines on the prowl,' the skipper warned quietly and the Berliner nodded. 'So you've got to pick up their radar probes before they locate us. Everything depends on you so keep on your toes.'

'Supposing they're using microwave scanners, sir? We can only pick up centimetre wavelengths on this gear.'

Bergman shot him a questioning glance. He thought only the top brass in the Kriegsmarine knew about the new Allied microwave radar sets. It never ceased to amaze him how well the lower deck kept themselves informed of such matters.

'Don't worry, Schwarze,' he said reassuringly. 'You can take it from me they aren't using microwave sets in the US Pacific Fleet yet - they're all going to Europe and the USAAF.'

He wished he felt as confident as he sounded. If the Yanks were using microwave radar then *U-885* had had it. Giving the *Metox* operator a cheerful slap on the back, he ducked through the bulkhead and walked aft.

Commander Fujita was sitting in the wardroom looking at a French magazine as Bergman slid the curtain open and entered. Holding up a large and voluptuous pin-up photograph of a leading Paris showgirl, he grinned across at the Kapitanleutnant.

'Big bits!' he pronounced eagerly.

Bergman glanced at the picture and grinned. Mitsu-ru's grasp of the English idiom was still a trifle precarious. But he knew what he meant. And, in many ways, it was an apt comment.

Despite the humid heat of the wardroom, Bergman still kept his favourite coffee pot simmering day and night. It was a habit he had started on *UB-44*'s first combat patrol and it was one he could not break. Lifting it up from the electric ring, he poured himself a cup of the poisonous-looking brew and settled himself down along-side his companion.

The time had come to reveal his hand to Fujita and to tell him the true purpose of *U-885*'s secret mission to Japan. He was going to need all the help he could get if the task was to be successfully completed and the Commander seemed the logical source of assistance.

Fujita listened impassively as Bergman outlined his instructions but the inscrutability of his expression gave no hint to his inner thoughts. The Kapitanleutnant made no mention of von Schiller's further instructions - there was no point in placing all his cards on the table. And in any case, Bergman was still undecided whether he would obey his alternative orders.

'I felt sure you had some ulterior motive in coming to Japan,' Fujita said slowly as Bergman finished. 'And I appreciate the honour you have done me in revealing your secret instructions.' He put the magazine down on the table and concentrated his thoughts. 'I wish I could be more hopeful but I am doubtful if your mission will meet with success.'

'Why? Germany and Japan are allies aren't they?'

'I suppose so.' Fujita shrugged. 'But it is an alliance I

have never really understood. How can Adolf Hitler accept our people as equals when he preaches the doctrine of racial supremacy - it is ridiculous.' He smiled suddenly. 'Please don't misunderstand me, Konrad. I realise that you do not support the Nazi regime just as I do not support the mad men who at present control Japan. But it is a fact we must both face.'

'Let's leave our political views out of it,' Bergman told him. After his experiences on *UB-44*, there was always a nagging doubt in his mind that *U-885* might also be harbouring a Gestapo spy. And in any case, he no longer admitted his true feelings to anyone. The part he intended to play in resolving Germany's destiny was now firmly formed in his mind and, for the moment, he intended to share his plans with no one. 'If we're giving the Tokyo admirals all our radar knowledge, why can't they exchange information about the *Type-93* torpedo?'

'You obviously do not understand the Japanese thought processes, Konrad. Secrecy is a national characteristic. And aside from that, why should your Admiral Doenitz want to know about our torpedo?'

'Because it's probably the finest weapon of its type in the world. If Germany had the Long Lance torpedo, our U-boats could wipe every enemy merchant ship off the face of the Atlantic inside a month.'

Fujita smiled to himself. He looked like a rotundly benign Buddha as he sat cross-legged on the lower bunk gently rocking himself backwards and forwards.

'If that is why you need the Long Lance, Konrad, then forget it. It is completely useless to you unless, of course, Germany is prepared to withdraw all her U-boats and rebuild them.' Bergman looked puzzled. Practically nothing was known about the oxygen-powered torpedo outside the Japanese Navy and Fujita's statement intrigued him.

'Why?' he demanded.

'Because the *Type-93* is a twenty-four-inch weapon and there's not a submarine in the world fitted with torpedo tubes larger than twenty-one-inch diameter. That's why even Japanese submarines are not equipped with the Long Lance - it's strictly a surface ship weapon.'

'But we could make it smaller - scale it down to twenty-one-inch diameter,' Bergman countered. 'Surely it would be a simple matter for our scientists.'

Fujita smiled again. 'I can see that our torpedo is an even greater secret than we imagined. Obviously your people have no idea of the problems associated with oxygen propulsion.' Bergman sipped his coffee slowly. Inside he felt as tense as a length of stretched elastic. Fujita obviously was not likely to blurt out the secret of the Long Lance but anything he revealed would provide a useful clue. And with luck it would enable him to bluff the Tokyo admirals into believing that Germany knew more about the torpedo than they had imagined. He tried to hide his eagerness as he waited.

'The difficulty about using oxygen as a propellant is its tendency to heat up under compression and explode,' Fujita explained. 'You will probably remember the characteristics from your chemistry lessons at school.'

Bergman shrugged. 'Not one of my best subjects,' he admitted ruefully. 'But I think I know what you're getting at.'

'You also know how cramped the inside of a torpedo is and how the fuel pipes twist and snake about all over the place.' Bergman nodded. He had good cause to be familiar with the working parts of the torpedo after *UB-44*'s last fatal dive.

'Because of this space problem,' Fujita continued, 'it is normal for the fuel lines to contain very sharp angles in them. But when Kishimoto and Asakuma began their experiments in the 'twenties, they found that the oxygen massed when it reached an acute bend, heated up as a result of the compression, and then exploded violently. No matter what systems they tried there seemed to be no way of escaping the problem until they discovered that the British Navy was experimenting on similar lines. And, more important, they found that the Royal Navy was using a twenty-four-point-five-inch diameter weapon.

'Fortunately, the British dropped the idea soon afterwards and switched to hydrogen peroxide. But our people suddenly realised that, by using a larger body shell, the kinks and angles in the fuel lines could be ironed out. And to cut a long story short, they finally succeeded in perfecting the system using a twenty-four-inch diameter weapon.'

'I see. So what you are saying is that you cannot use an oxygen propellant in a torpedo with a smaller diameter than twenty-four inches.'

'Precisely, my friend. And as all your U-boats are fitted with twenty-one-inch tubes, the *Type-93* would be completely useless unless larger tubes were fitted. And that would be an impractical solution at this period of the war.'

For the first time since his interview with Doenitz, Bergman began to consider his arrival in Japan with a less jaundiced eye. Fujita was right. The entire project was an utter waste of time for Germany's U-boats. And that meant, he thought maliciously, that von Schiller's orders to steal the plans could be ignored with impunity.

Reaching up, he pulled open the locker, and brought out one of the bottles of dimple Haig that Fujita had thoughtfully brought aboard with him. Yoko's little bronze casket wobbled as he slammed the door shut and he tried not to think of its contents. Pouring the whisky into his empty coffee cup, Berg man took a deep gulp and felt it burning his throat.

'You don't know how helpful you've been, Mitsuru.' He held out the bottle. 'Have some of this and help me celebrate.'

Fujita shook his head politely. 'Thank you, but no. I prefer Saki. And as I'm due on watch in an hour or so, I prefer to remain clear-headed.' He was puzzled by Bergman's eagerness to celebrate. He could not imagine why the Kapitanleutnant was so pleased to discover that *Type-93* was of no practical use; it was a strange reaction for a man who had travelled halfway around the world to acquire its secrets.

'But we do have something that should interest your Admiral Doenitz,' he added after a pause.

'What's that?'

Fujita's expression was enigmatic but he looked rather like a little boy trying hard not to reveal a secret. 'You will see . . . you will see. From your point of view, it will probably be of far more practical value than the *Type-93*. And an old friend of mine is in charge of the project.'

'So when do I get to see it?'

'When we get to Japan. Once you've finished in Tokyo, I'll take you down to Sasebo. You won't be able to resist it when...'

The warning squawk of the diving klaxon cut him off

in mid-sentence and as Bergman rose to his feet, he felt *U-885* dig her nose down in a steeply angled dive.

'Captain to the control room!'

The throb of the diesels had faded away and the soft hum of the motors had replaced the roar of the main engines. Bergman could hear the sea flooding into the ballast tanks as the main vents opened and the needle of the depth-gauge was already swinging towards the 20-feet calibration mark.

'Schwarze picked up a radar probe, sir,' von Schroeder explained as Bergman joined him at the periscope. 'I dived immediately in accordance with your Standing Orders.'

'Quite correct, Number One. Better safe than sorry. Was it an aircraft?'

'No, sir. Konstam also picked up HE on his phones at the same time.'

Bergman grasped the periscope handles and slid his bottom onto the saddle seat. He peered through the eyepieces and carefully checked through the full 360° arc of the horizon.

'Nothing in sight,' he grunted. He leaned across and flicked the intercom switch linking him with Schwarze. 'Are you sure you picked up radar impulses?'

'Yes, sir. Positive response - strength seven.'

Bergman cleared the switch and depressed another. 'Report on HE, Konstam.'

'A bit of a puzzle, sir.'

'I'll do the theorising, Konstam,' Bergman snapped. 'Just give me the facts.'

'I located very faint diesel engine noises - range about three miles if it was a big ship. Considerably less if it was small.'

'Any of your boats using diesels, Commander?'
Bergman called down to Fujita who was standing in the
control room below.

'No - only our submarines.'

'Continue your report, Konstam.'

'Well, just about the time Schwarze picked up the
radar pulses on his *Metox*, the HE faded out. Then there
were a lot of water noises. About two minutes later, I
heard electric motor sounds - range two miles and
approaching on the starboard bow.'

'Do we still have them?'

'Yes, sir. Closing at about four knots.'

Bergman reacted immediately. 'Full right rudder -
hard a'dive! Full ahead motors.'

'Group up! Full ahead both!'

'Planes at maximum diving angle, sir.'

'Full starboard helm, sir.'

U-885 corkscrewed towards the depths as the
propellers kicked her to maximum submerged speed. Her
bows swung around in response to the rudder until they
were pointing directly towards the unknown threat of HE
creeping slowly towards them.

'Stop motors! Rig for silent running.'

Badenholdt passed the message to the motor room
and Venne reached up, pulled the main switch, and killed
the humming motors. Throughout the length of the U-
boat, men shut down auxiliary equipment and cut off the
sucking squelch of the bilge pumps. An uncanny quiet
descended on the U-boat as she drifted silently through
the water.

No one spoke a word but questioning glances were
exchanged as the men tried to discern the reason for the
skipper's sudden emergency action. Obviously something

nasty was about to happen. But why the hell had he stopped the motors and left them suspended in the grey-green depths halfway between the surface and the ocean bottom? Why hadn't he turned on full power and high-tailed out of trouble?

Obergefrieter Konstam hunched over his listening equipment as he strained to pick up another clue through his earphones. Reaching towards the control panel, he used both hands to turn the knobs as if he were trying to tune into a fading radio station.

'Sir.'

His voice, pitched in a low whisper, sounded urgent.

Bergman had forsaken his lonely perch in the conning-tower command room and was standing directly behind the hydrophone operator.

'What is it, Korman?'

'High-pitched propeller noises approaching dead ahead - speed about forty knots.'

Bergman's mouth went dry. For the first time in his life, he had been snared in an underwater ambush and the utter defencelessness of *U-885* sent a shiver tingling down his spine.

'Five hundred yards, sir. Four ... three ... two ...'

Konstam's monotonous calling off of the range added to the tension inside the submarine. It was like the hangman counting down the seconds before springing the trap door under the prisoner's feet. Beads of sweat glistened on the faces of the waiting men and tongues reached out to moisten dry lips. Bergman heard a soft movement behind his back and, turning his head, he saw Fujita. The Japanese Commander was as calmly impassive as ever. Like Bergman, he had also realised the meaning of the hydrophone noises and the radar contact and with typical oriental fatalism, he accepted that the Kapitanleutnant had done all he could. It was now in the hands of the gods.

The sound of the whirring torpedo propellers lancing through the water was now clearly audible inside the U-boat without the aid of *U-885's* listening devices and for a few seconds it was as if every man inside the submarine had stopped breathing.

Then suddenly the whirring sounds crescendoed to a climax of volume and began fading into the distance. Every man released his pent-up breath at the same moment. Death had passed them by and they made no secret of their relief.

The torpedoes had passed directly above *U-885's* hull, miraculously missing the jumping wires and other impedimenta that cluttered the bridge and conning tower, and they would now speed aimlessly into the empty wastes of the ocean until their air reservoirs were exhausted and they sank harmlessly to the bottom.

Hartmann wiped the sweat from his face and glanced across at Bottcher. He wasn't quite sure what had happened but it was obvious from the skipper's expression that they'd had a narrow escape.

'You can stop shitting your pants, Max!' he shouted to Bottcher. 'It's all over.'

'Silence!'

Bergman's sharp reprimand reawakened the tension inside the U-boat. Like Willi Hartmann, most of the crew thought the danger was over. But obviously the skipper knew otherwise. What the hell was going on?

'Was it one of yours?' Bergman asked Fujita.

'No - the engines were running faster than our models. And bearing in mind the radar pulse that

Schwarze detected, I'm quite sure it wasn't from a Japanese vessel.'

None of the crew spoke English sufficiently well to understand the significance of the snatched question and answer. Bergman noticed the puzzled expressions on their faces and decided it was time to let them into the secret. Leaning forward and speaking quietly, he told them to pass the information back down the boat to the other members of the crew.

'We seem to be under attack by another submarine - almost certainly an American,' he explained. 'They must have spotted us on the surface with their radar and, so far as I can judge, we both dived simultaneously. But the enemy had got our bearings and he took a blind shot at us with a couple of torpedoes in the anticipation that we were maintaining our course, speed, and depth. That is why I cut the engines. Radar can't operate underwater so, like us, he's now restricted to carrying out a listening watch on his hydrophones. We're both groping about in the dark hoping the other will give his position away - it's rather like two blind men playing darts in a moving car.'

Fujita nodded as Bergman explained the situation. He admired the Kapitanleutnant's reassuring words. Very comforting. But as an ex-submariner himself, he was only too aware that Bergman had chosen to paint his situation report in optimistic colours in order to bolster morale.

In the old days, his explanation would have contained more than a germ of truth. With only the sensitive ears of their listening devices to help them locate their adversary, both submarines would have been equally blind. In those days, skill and cunning were at a premium. And even more important, either boat had an equal chance of success.

But not any more. What Bergman had failed to tell *U-885*'s men was that the American submarine now stalking them through the turgid green depths of the South China Sea was fitted with a sonar device that could transmit sound underwater and pick up the echoes of any submerged object within range. And that weighted the odds heavily in favour of the enemy.

'What do we do now, sir?' von Schroeder asked quietly.

'We wait,' Bergman whispered back. 'We wait until the enemy's nerve cracks and he tries to escape. The moment his motors start, Korman will pick up the sounds on his phones. And I shall launch a submerged attack.'

FIVE

'Stop motors, Mr. Hagon. Secure for silent running.'

The vibrating hum of the electric motors died away and USS *Needlefish* drifted like a grey-green ghost as the current swept her forward at a funereal two knots. The men sitting at the diving controls relaxed and tried to occupy their minds with thoughts a thousand miles away from the underwater ambush in which they had become embroiled. Further aft, lying in their narrow bunks, the off-duty Watch dozed fitfully.

Lieutenant-Commander Satterlee had long since stopped counting off the seconds of elapsed time. The torpedoes had missed and the main chance had gone. It could have happened to anyone but it was damnably annoying when it happened to you. He nodded for the First Officer to join him at the chart-table and he kept his voice low.

'You're quite sure none of our boats are operating in this area, Number One?'

'Affirmative, sir.' Lieutenant (jg) Hagon was only six months out of Annapolis and the newfound weight of responsibility had given him a premature maturity that belied his twenty years. Just two combat patrols as Third Hand - and one of those in a 'pig-boat' that hadn't ventured more than two hundred miles from Pearl Harbor - and here he was second-in-command of one of the latest *Gato* class patrol submarines. 'I checked CINPAC's Fleet Orders and the Flotilla patrol roster. There's not a friendly submarine within five hundred miles of this goddamned spot.'

'How about Dutch? They're working out of Darwin aren't they?'

'Yes, but their patrol limit is south and east of the Philippines and Borneo. The Dutch haven't operated in the China Seas since they lost Java.'

Satterlee rubbed his hands across his face as he tried to resolve the doubts in his mind. 'I could swear it was no Jap submarine I spotted. That was the smartest piece of diving I've seen in many a long day.'

'But if it wasn't a Jap boat, sir, what the hell could it be? There's nothing else in the area.'

The skipper was scarcely listening. He knew perfectly well that *Needlefish* was the only allied submarine on patrol in the South China Sea which was why he'd attacked immediately when they'd obtained radar contact. But, cautious as ever, he preferred to double check.

'It looked exactly like a German U-boat,' he said slowly as if doubting the evidence of his own eyes. 'And how the hell can you meet up with a Kraut submarine in the middle of the China Sea?'

Satterlee had caught only a fleeting glimpse of the mystery submarine as it dived but it was enough to chase any lingering doubts from his mind. And there were other significant facts to confirm his first conclusion.

The enemy had dived so swiftly she must have detected the radar probe. In fact, she had started diving a full fifteen seconds before they'd made visual contact. And so far as Satterlee knew, only German U-boats were equipped with radar detectors - the Nips were much too far behind in the technology race to possess such sophisticated devices.

But what worried Satterlee even more was the knowledge that his opponent was an extremely skilful submarine commander. The U-boat had been a sitting target and yet, somehow, her skipper had twisted her out of the path of the torpedoes with the agility of a trained seal performing at a circus. And he'd never seen a Jap move that quickly. But what the hell was a German U-boat doing off the coast of Sarawak?

'Any HE?' he asked Henderson, the senior signaller sitting at the hydrophone listening apparatus.

'No, sir. Not a sound. Reckon he's killed his engines same as us.'

'Mitchell! Switch on the Sonar. Start searching on bearing 3-0-0 and scan forty-five degrees either side.'

'Sonar on, sir. Bearing Three-Zero-Zero. Commencing search.'

Satterlee had no way of knowing whether U-boats could detect the underwater pulses of a Sonar probe but it was a chance he had to take. He might be betraying his own position but there was no alternative.

'Sonar echoes bearing three-two-five, sir! '

Mitchell glanced up to find Satterlee leaning over his shoulders and peering down at the instrument console. 'What do you make of it, Sam?' he asked.

'It's a positive contact, sir.' Mitchell cocked his head to one side as he tried to decipher the echoes in his earphones. 'Very narrow area of contact, though. And bloody close.'

'How close?'

'I'd say not more than two hundred yards - target probably end-on.'

Satterlee could almost picture the scene taking place in the murky depths of the South China Sea. The two submarines, silent and inert like lifeless pieces of wood, floating almost motionless below the surface yet drifting gently from the momentum of their now dead engines and at the mercy of the current sweeping down from the Balabac Strait to the north.

Judging by Mitchell's report, *Needlefish* was lying broadside onto the unidentified submarine - the most dangerous position it was possible to be in. If the Kraut had any sort of detection devices on board, Satterlee knew his boat was wallowing helplessly like a sitting duck directly ahead of the enemy's torpedo tubes at point-blank range. A bead of sweat trickled slowly down his face.

He gave Mitchell long enough to measure the increase or decrease in the intervals between the probe and the echo.

'Approaching or receding?' he asked anxiously.

Not that it made any difference, he reminded himself grimly. Most modern submarines were fitted with torpedo tubes in both stern and bows and *Needlefish* was lying broadside to the enemy's line of axis.

'Approaching, sir. Must be drifting though. Speed not much above two knots.' Mitchell suddenly reached forward and twisted desperately at the knobs on his control panel. 'Shit! Of all the bloody stupid ...'

He checked himself abruptly as he remembered the skipper standing behind him. 'Sonar malfunction, sir,' he reported apologetically. 'I think it's a burned-out valve.'

'How long to fix it?'

'Three or four minutes, sir.' Mitchell reached for a screwdriver to open up the control panel and twisted round in his seat. 'Hey, Charlie! Get down to the electrical stores and bring me up an FX-Nineteen!'

His urgent yell echoed around the control room like the voice of an undisciplined schoolboy shouting in the nave of an empty cathedral.

'Button it!' snapped Satterlee. 'Just keep your mouth shut and fix that damned box-of-tricks.' He swung away from the sonar station angrily and joined Hagon at the diving panel.

'SOUNDS DEAD AHEAD, SIR.'

Bergman was alongside Korman almost before anyone else on board U-885 had realised the significance of the whispered report.

'Range?'

'Difficult to say, sir. Probably a couple of hundred yards - no more. It sounded like someone shouting an order.'

Bergman snapped his fingers as he swung around to von Schroeder. There was always that crucial moment in every action when the vital decision had to be taken. And inevitably there was always insufficient information on which to base a rational command. But with the sixth sense on which every combat submarine commander relied, Bergman had a sudden vision of the two submarines drifting towards each other fifty feet below the surface.

'Motors on! Full ahead both!'

Badenholdt instinctively held the mouthpiece of his telephone closer to his lips to ensure no misunderstanding of the vital order.

'Switches on! Group up - full ahead both!'

Suddenly the entire boat came alive. Venne pulled the main switch and then moved the heavy insulated grouper lever to full power. The motors responded instantly and the ammeters flickered to maximum discharge as the current was sucked from the battery cells deep below the steel plating of the main deck. The entire hull vibrated and even the fans were unable to disperse the sickly-sweet smell of ozone that filled the motor room and wafted forward into the control room.

'Full ahead both, Chief.'

Venne's report was almost superfluous. *U-885* tucked her stem down as the bronze propellers thrust into the water and urged her forward.

'Stand by collision stations! Close all watertight doors. Evacuate forward torpedo flat!'

The heavy rubber-sealed doors slammed shut as the men locked and clipped the two levers and *U-885* was turned into a series of isolated tin boxes - each section cut off from its neighbour by the thick steel bulkheads that divided the submarine into eight self-contained water-tight compartments. Only the snaking yellow-painted cables of the internal communication system maintained contact between them. And even that was reserved for the skipper's exclusive use.

Bergman lifted the phone and called up the fore-ends section. 'Report please.'

'Bow torpedo compartment secured, sir,' Manhaussen acknowledged. 'Number Two door shut and clipped - all men evacuated.'

He handed the instrument to Torpedomechaniker Vame who was making frantic signals. 'The bow tubes are still loaded, sir!'

'The detonator safety pins?'

'In position and secured, sir.'

'Very good, Vame. Let's hope the bows stand up to the impact without crumpling or we'll all be blown to kingdom come. Tell your lads to hang on tight.'

The red second hand of the brass rimmed chronometer set high on the white painted wall of the control room swept into its third minute and every man clung tightly to his chosen support and braced his body to resist the jolt of the impending collision.

Moments later, U-885 shuddered to an abrupt stop and the shriek of torn metal echoed through the hull like the wail of an agonised banshee. With her propellers still thrusting forward at maximum revolutions, the U-boat ground her sharp nose into the vulnerable ballast tanks of Needlefish and there were harsh grinding noises as the two submarines wrestled for survival below the surface like a pair of primeval sea monsters locked in a life-and-death struggle for control of the ocean floor.

'Blow Bow One and Two!'

High-pressure air screeched through the lines as the control valves spun open. U-885's bows rose upwards and forced her opponent down into the depths as she slid over the enemy's foredeck casing.

Satterlee was thrown full-length on the floor of the

control room as the U-boat sliced into *Needlefish's* fragile ballast tanks and as he picked himself up, the submarine tilted violently to port, rolled back with a sickening lurch, and then heeled over again. It was like a rat being gripped in a terrier's jaws and violently shaken. The lights went out and men cursed and struggled in the darkness.

'Switches on! Full astern both!'

Knevet tried to ignore the terrifying noise of water flooding into the hull as he groped for the emergency lighting controls. A vivid blue spark flashed across the main fuses and there was an acrid smell of burning rubber in his nostrils. Locating the switch, he jerked it down and the dim red glow of the reserve lighting restored order from chaos as the crew found their bearings.

Chief Electrician Pilsudski, stolid and imperturbable as always, carefully isolated a smoking power cable, checked the row of dials over his control position and then, with a silent prayer to his patron saint, pulled the main switch down. There was an instant response from the motors and *Needlefish* shuddered and groaned as she dragged herself wearily from under the keel of the U-boat.

'Tort motor burned out, sir!'

Satterlee acknowledged Pilsudski's report curtly as he tried to weigh up the situation. *Needlefish* was crippled - that was for certain. And in hostile water, two thousand miles from base, their position was desperate. The stem was already swinging to starboard as the submarine pivoted on its dead propeller and despite the reassuring glow of the green lights on the diving panel, Ensign Taylor had reported serious leaks in both bow compartments. Even worse, the periscopes were damaged and the submarine was completely blind.

'Stand by to surface. We're going topsides to fight it out!'

'Blow all tanks - hydroplanes hard a-rise. Gun crews close up!'

Despite his inexperience, Hagon was as cool as his skipper and Satterlee thanked his lucky stars for the blessing of a good crew.

'Ten feet, sir.'

Satterlee scrambled up the ladder and opened the lower hatch. Pausing for a moment, he glanced down at the anxious faces of the men waiting to follow him on deck.

'I don't intend to surrender, men, and I want that gun in action as soon as we break surface. If any of you fancy ending up in a Jap prison camp, you're welcome. But I intend to fight this ship until the enemy is beaten or she sinks under my feet. Now let's get to hell or glory!'

Reaching upwards, Satterlee slid the clips of the upper hatch and thrust it open.

U-885, having surfaced two minutes earlier, was already impatiently quartering the area like a lion pacing eagerly round its victim and Bergman felt the tension rising as they waited. In his own mind, he was certain his opponent was crippled but equally he realised that if he was wrong, the U-boat, exposed and naked as she prowled the surface, was at the mercy of a submerged torpedo attack.

Standing alongside him at the bridge rails, Fujita seemed as unconcerned as ever. Yet behind the impassive mask lay a new respect for *U-885*'s skipper.

Until now, he had been convinced that only Japanese sailors had the courage to commit suicide to achieve victory. But Bergman's shock decision to ram the enemy submarine had led him to a hasty revision of his previous opinions and he began to understand why the Kapitan-leutnant had built up his brilliant reputation as a combat submarine commander.

Incredibly they had survived the underwater collision and now, unless Bergman had miscalculated, they were about to become involved in an even more desperate battle in which one of the protagonists must be destroyed. Patting the traditional cotton belt drawn tightly around his waist, Fujita hoped that the old superstitions still held good.

The sea on the port side of *U-885* began heaving convulsively. Giant bubbles of air rose to the surface and burst with a faintly ludicrous pop. The green of the water turned to grey as a million tiny bubbles raced upwards in the wake of the original eruption and a cauldron of white foam boiled to the surface. Bergman gripped the bridge stanchions more tightly and watched eagerly for his first glimpse of the unknown enemy rising up from the depths to give battle.

'Stand by!'

Neisser, *U-885*'s warrant gunner, acknowledged the warning command. The deck gun crew was already at their battle stations and Willi Hartmann, as reserve gunlayer, spun the traversing wheel to swing the questing barrel in line with the centre of the disturbed water. This was his big chance to prove that the Penang incident was not just a flash in the pan. Licking his lips with anticipation, he squinted down the sight and waited.

Fujita, too, found the excitement infectious and he grinned across at von Schroeder who responded with a thumbs-up signal. Bergman alone seemed unaffected by the proximity of battle. Taciturn and calm, he waited patiently for the enemy to emerge from its underwater lair. Without moving his eyes from the frothing caudron of water, he bent over the engine room voice pipe.

'Maintain slow ahead, Chief, but stand by for emergency full power if I give the word.'

"Enemy surfacing on port beam!'

Bergman raised his head as the lookout shouted his warning. Less than 600 yards away, the sharply-angled bow of a submarine poked up through the soapsuds lather, dipped below the surface and then emerged again, streaming water from her drain holes.

Needlefish lurched and rolled as she regained surface trim and Bergman could see the gaping rent in her forward ballast tanks where *U-885's* bows had cut deeply into the steel plating. Black oil was pulsing from a fractured fuel line like lifeblood pumping from a severed artery and he knew his enemy was hopelessly crippled. For a brief moment, compassion - an emotion which Bergman had not realised he still possessed - brought *Needlefish* a short reprieve from death as he held fire. It was his first and only error of judgement. Taking advantage of the unexpected respite, the American sailors scrambled up through the hatch and dashed down the deck towards the forward 6-inch gun.

'Three rounds rapid - *fire!*'

It was not too late to retrieve the situation but Bergman cursed himself for showing mercy to an enemy he had yet to beat in open battle. Fortunately, he still retained the vital advantage of being at action stations. But it was an advantage that would be wiped out as soon as *Needlefish* got her guns working.

Neisser squeezed the firing-lever and *U-885's* 88mm recoiled smoothly. Moving quickly despite his bulk,

Bottcher jerked down the breech lever and the still smoking cartridge shot from the empty breech, struck the steel deck plating and bounced into the sea with a hiss of quenched hot metal. Meyer thrust a second Mk VII HE into the hungry orifice and stepped back smartly as Bottcher locked the breech lever down.

The first shell fell ten yards short and Hartmann swung the gun-sight ten feet to the right of his abortive ranging shot and elevated the barrel three degrees.

'Fire!'

This time, he was on target and a sheet of yellow flame seared up from the base of the conning tower as the shell exploded.

'Knock out the gun!' Bergman yelled from the bridge.

Hartmann's hands obediently reversed their movement and he swung back towards the bows of the enemy. The skipper was right. If the gun wasn't silenced, they wouldn't stand a chance against the American's heavier metal. The bark of a machine gun shattered the air behind him and Willi ducked involuntarily as the bullets screamed over his head towards the enemy submarine. Losing his concentration, he glanced around.

Fujita was grinning broadly as he tucked the Spandau deeper into his shoulder and fired another burst at the exposed American gunners. He cut down two of them and chased a third back towards the conning tower with bullets ripping the deck at his heels as he ran. But, defying the machine-gun fire, the gun crew's three survivors continued their struggle to get the weapon into action. Fujita slammed a fresh clip of cartridges into the Spandau, sighted at the shattered bridge, and moved his attack to a fresh quarter.

'Down! Take cover!'

Satterlee ducked behind the bridge screen as he shouted the warning. But it was too late to save Hagon. Fujita's bullets thudded into the lieutenant's back and threw him against the periscope mounting. He paused for a moment and then slid slowly to the deck in a crumpled heap. His hands clenched and opened in a spasm of unendurable pain and then he went limp.

Boatswain First Class Erwin Frapp kept low as he picked his way through the smoking wreckage of the bridge. His right arm, shattered above the elbow, hung uselessly at his side and blood was streaming down his face from a jagged splinter wound across his forehead. Edging carefully past the lieutenant's body, he joined the skipper crouching behind the screen.

'Guess we ought to throw in the towel, sir. There's only two left alive on the bridge. If she goes down under our feet, the whole goddamned crew will be trapped inside.'

'We keep fighting, bos'n,' Satterlee told him grimly. 'That kraut skipper won't want to risk having his boat damaged and if we can get the deck gun into action, I think we can fight them off. Send more men topsides.' He raised his head to peer over the bridge screen but ducked quickly as Fujita's machine gun opened up again. 'Get a move on, man!'

But despite his brave words, Satterlee knew the situation was hopeless. The U-boat's anti-aircraft pom-pom, firing at its lowest elevation, had joined in the massacre and not a single man of the deck gun crew survived this new onslaught. The German gunners had the range precisely and any further attempt to get the six-incher into action was an invitation to mass suicide. The submarine was slowly settling by the head and was noticeably lower in the water. Yet even in the face of the fast increasing odds, Satterlee refused to accept defeat. Belly-crawling to the hatch, he stuck his head down inside the circular opening.

'Hard left rudder, Cox'n! And pass the word back to the Chief to give me maximum power ahead.'

If the Kraut could ram him underwater, Satterlee saw no reason why he should not reciprocate the compliment on the surface. In any event, it was the only chance he had left.

'Sir, the Chief says the engines are dead. He's working on them but it'll take time.'

The report, muffled and hollow as it echoed up through the vault of the lower conning tower, reached Satterlee like the voice of doom. Dragging himself away from the hatch, he made his way back to the port side and lay flat on the deck plating as Fujita's bullets buzzed and whined around his head like angry hornets.

Needlefish answered the helm sluggishly. Dipping lower into the sea as water flooded her forward compartment, her crumpled bows turned slowly and painfully towards the U-boat in a gallantly defiant attempt to turn the tide of battle. Satterlee prayed that she'd make it but the gods of war were deaf to his entreaties.

U-885's third shell struck the submarine directly beneath the unmanned deck gun. *Needlefish* kicked like a wounded elephant and a jagged lump of splintered steel, red hot from the detonation, smashed into the box of ready-for-use ammunition a few feet from the gun. A thunderclap explosion split the air and a sheet of yellow flame clawed high into the sky as the entire contents went up.

Needlefish snapped into two pieces and slipped

slowly back into the sea. The bows disappeared beneath the surface within seconds and as the conning-tower section lingered agonisingly before its final plunge, the crew fought and struggled to escape through the narrow hatch. Ripped and torn by the explosion, their uniforms hanging in charred tatters and their faces blackened by the acrid smoke that filled the hull, they resembled a group of survivors from a mining disaster.

'Cease fire!' Bergman lowered his head over the control-room voice pipe. 'Hard right rudder. Slow ahead starboard.'

U-885 circled to the right to bring the remains of Needlefish onto her lee side.

'Stand by to recover survivors.'

Hartmann heaved himself out of the gunlayer's seat with a weary sigh, dropped to the deck, and joined Bottcher and the other fore-end's men on the bow casing. The enemy submarine had vanished beneath the surface within twenty seconds of the final explosions and only an ugly reeking circle of fuel oil marked her grave. Five heads bobbed in the centre of the black sludge and U-885's deck party crouched, waiting on the ballast tanks as Bergman steered into the evil mess. The choking oil fumes made their eyes water but, ignoring their discomfort and clinging grimly to the safety lines, the U-boatmen leaned out to grab the exhausted survivors from the sea.

'Stop engines.'

Three bodies, blackened with oil, floated face down as the U-boat drifted slowly with the current but Bergman's expressionless face showed no trace of emotion. It could just as easily have been U-885's fate if luck had not been on his side. That was the way it had to be in war. And if another enemy ship appeared on the horizon, he knew he would abandon the survivors to their fate without the slightest twinge of conscience.

One of the U-boatmen caught an upraised arm, gripped firmly, and dragged an exhausted sailor to the safety of *U-885*'s deck. Two more followed, then another, but the fifth suddenly vanished beneath the surface before they could reach him.

'There's another one - ten yards off the bow!'

Hartmann could not understand Fujita's shouted report to Bergman for, in the excitement of battle, Mitsuru had lapsed back into his native tongue. But there was no mistaking what he meant and Willi's eyes followed the direction of the Commander's pointing finger.

The poor bastard had nearly had it. He was kicking at the oil-scummed water but the glutinous black sludge was restricting his arms and Hartmann could see the man's eyes staring hopelessly towards them as they drifted down current beyond his reach. They were too close to circle towards him and Hartmann knew that Bergman would need to take *U-885* in a wide sweep in order to bring her alongside. And it was obvious that the exhausted man couldn't hold out that long.

Willi looked down at the blackened sea and swallowed hard. The American raised an arm weakly to attract attention and he knew he couldn't stand by and watch him drown in that foul-smelling filth. Stripping off his shirt, Hartmann slipped and slithered down the bulging curve of the starboard ballast tank and dived into the evil-looking slime.

He reached Satterlee in a dozen strokes, crooked his arm around the man's throat, and kicked backwards to haul him back to the U-boat. The fumes choked his throat and clogged his nose. His eyes stung as the oil splashed his face and he could feel his muscles tiring as he fought to break free of the sucking black sludge.

Bottcher reached down and, helped by Beitzen, hauled the semi-conscious Satterlee onto the deck while Hartmann climbed back up the ballast tank looking like a Stygian sea monster emerging from a mud bath. He was still recovering his breath when the contents of a bucket caught him full in the stomach and bowled him over onto the foredeck casing as Manhaussen sluiced the worst of the oil from his body. It was an undignified way to welcome a hero but Willi managed a weak grin.

'Secure for diving! All hands below!'

Leaning his elbows on the conning-tower coaming, Bergman watched the survivors coming aft. One, at least, was in a bad way. Semi-conscious and oozing blood from an ugly wound in his stomach, he was groaning softly as Botcher and Neisser carried him in an improvised stretcher. The others, still blackened and blinded by oil scum, were guided gently through the deck-level hatch on the port side of the conning tower where Konstam and Siess were waiting to help them down the final ladder.

Satterlee brought up the rear of the pathetic procession. He stopped when he came level with the bridge and looked up. Despite his exhaustion, he found the strength to salute his opponent.

'Thank you for saving my men, Kapitanleutnant.'

For once in his life, Bergman felt embarrassed. He had done no more than his duty and he was only too aware of the other occasions when operational necessity had forced him to leave his victims to their fate. The American officer's blue and gold shoulder boards were just visible through the black sludge saturating his khaki uniform.

'You fought a good fight, Lieutenant Commander,' he acknowledged gruffly. 'Now get below, please. We are about to submerge.'

Satterlee hesitated and then obediently ducked through the conning-tower hatch. His initial bewilderment at meeting up with a German U-boat in the middle of the South China Sea redoubled as he glimpsed Fujita standing on the bridge behind *U-885*'s skipper.

'Hands to diving stations! Clear the bridge!'

The klaxon squawked its final warning and the U-boat was already digging its bows under the surface as Bergman lowered himself down the conning-tower ladder and pulled the hatch clips.

'What do you propose to do with the prisoners?' Fujita asked as they settled back on the leather benches in the wardroom. Bergman shrugged.

'Take them to Tokyo, I suppose. It's a problem we don't often encounter in U-boats,' he added a trifle defensively.

'But it will take well over a week to reach Japan,' the Commander pointed out. 'They will have vital information in their possession. If we handed them over to our Navy intelligence officers within the next twenty-four hours, it would be better than waiting a week to question them.'

For some reason, Bergman had never thought of prisoners in that light before. In the Atlantic combat zone, few of the survivors had any information likely to assist the U-boat High Command and in any case, they rarely revealed more than their name, rank, and number. *BdU* had its own sources of intelligence and, in the majority of circumstances, often knew more than the enemy it hunted so relentlessly. Germany had broken a number of British naval codes and by skilful monitoring of enemy radio transmissions, the wolf packs could be directed to Allied convoys without the assistance, willing or unwilling, of prisoners.

Bergman poured himself a cup of coffee as he considered the matter. A strange lurking doubt in his mind warned him not to follow Fujita's advice. He couldn't explain it but he had a premonition of tragedy.

'I can't spare the fuel for a diversion,' he said finally. 'And delivering prisoners isn't part of my mission. They'll have to come to Japan with us and I'll hand them over to your people as soon as we dock.'

Fujita shrugged. Despite his apparent westernisation, he still retained his primitive samurai instincts. To surrender or be taken prisoner was an act of dishonour in his eyes and, so far as he was concerned, the American survivors were of no consequence save as sources of information. And if the information was over a week old, it would be virtually useless. But it was Bergman's boat and the decision was his. He had at least lived long enough in the western world to understand the reservations in his companion's mind.

'Sir.'

Bergman looked up. Sanitasobermaat Hoyt was standing at the parted curtains that screened the wardroom.

'What is it, Hoyt?'

'It's the American prisoners, sir. One of them won't last more than six or seven hours without surgery. He needs urgent hospital facilities.'

'Thank you, Hoyt. Do your best to make him comfortable and I'll see what can be arranged. And have the officer brought to the wardroom.'

Satterlee was escorted from the forward torpedo room which had been hastily adapted for the use of the unwounded prisoners. He seemed surprised to find Fujita sitting with Bergman and, pointedly ignoring his presence, he saluted the Kapitanleutnant.

'Please sit down, Lieutenant Commander,' Bergman told him quietly. 'I hope you are being adequately looked after.'

Satterlee nodded and accepting the invitation, sat down on the leather bench that ran along the starboard bulkhead of the wardroom. He looked pale and exhausted from his ordeal and despite Hoyt's attention's, the roots of his hair were still caked in black oil sludge. Someone had given him a pair of fatigue trousers two sizes too small and Bottcher had donated a sweatshirt that enveloped him like a sack. In any other circumstances, it would have been a ludicrous combination.

Bergman passed over the gist of Hoyt's report. 'Commander Fujita tells me there is a Japanese army camp on Balabac Island. It lies directly on our course and we will reach it in two hours or so. There are hospital and surgical facilities at the base. I can hand you and your men over to the Army commandant or you can remain on board until we reach our destination. I leave the decision to you.'

'Is your destination Europe, Kapitanleutnant?'

Bergman hesitated. He did not like giving things away to the enemy but, in the circumstances, there seemed no harm in revealing the truth. He shook his head. 'We are en route to Japan, Lieutenant Commander.'

Satterlee bit his lip as he weighed the alternatives. He

attached no blame to Bergman - the U-boat skipper was only doing his job.

'To be honest, Kapitanleutnant, either way we face torture and probable execution.'

'Rubbish!' Bergman snapped. 'As prisoners of war, you are protected by the Geneva Convention. You should not believe the propaganda your government fabricates on the radio. They say exactly the same sort of thing about our German prison camps and you have my personal assurance that it is all a tissue of lies.' Even as he spoke, Bergman suddenly recalled his last meeting with Rahel Youssof after the Gestapo had finished with her. But, he reminded himself, the Nazis were to blame for that - not the German people.

'Believe me, sir, it's not propaganda - it's the goddamn truth!' Satterlee nodded towards Fujita. 'Ask him.'

Bergman glanced across at the Commander. He said nothing but waited for Fujita's denial.

'We treat prisoners as prisoners should be treated.' His eyes smouldered darkly. 'The Code of the Bushido is worth a hundred Geneva Conventions. An honourable man need have no fears as to his treatment by the Imperial Navy or the Japanese army.'

It was obvious from the expression on Satterlee's face what he thought of Fujita's statement. Having served in Shanghai when the Japanese took over the city before the war, he knew what happened to prisoners. Even Bergman felt slightly uneasy but he dismissed the fears from his mind.

'Well, Lieutenant Commander?' he asked. 'The choice is yours. There are hospital facilities at Balabac and my medical orderly considers that your men need urgent surgical attention. Do I land you or do I take you on to Japan?

Satterlee stood up. He wondered whether Bergman was really ignorant of Japanese methods. 'You must do as you decide best, Kapitanleutnant. We all knew we were signing our death warrants the moment we surrendered.'

SIX

Having taken his decision to land the prisoners at Balabac and hand them over to the army garrison, Bergman washed any lingering doubts from his mind. His philosophy of life was simple and direct. Once committed to a course of action, see it through to the bitter end. It was too late to worry in any case.

And right now the delicate task of conning *U-885* over the treacherous razor-sharp coral reefs that fringed Balabac's northern lagoon was the only thing that concerned him.

'Shoals to starboard,' Fujita warned. Sitting cross-legged on the floor of the bridge, his stubby finger carefully traced their course on the British Admiralty chart spread out on the deck in front of him.

Von Schroeder's task was to watch the echo-sounder and at every alteration in depth report the figures to the skipper. 'Twenty feet... eighteen feet...'

'One point to port, Steuermann.' Bergman's voice reflected none of the tension he felt as he groped his way into the unknown harbour. He sounded as if he were exercising in the familiar waters of Kiel Bay. 'Engines - dead slow ahead.'

Deep down in the control room, Holst acknowledged the order and moved the helm one point. Further aft in the engine room the repeater telegraph pinged as Aachan reduced the throttles of the MAN diesels to minimum revolutions. *U-885* swung her bows gently towards the tiny wooden pier jutting out from the beach and the throbbing power of her engines faded to a soft rumble.

'Sixteen feet... fifteen feet..

'Shallow water twenty yards ahead, Konrad.'

Bergman nodded. 'Stop engines! Let go bow anchors.'

A clattering roar from the bows followed by a cloud of red dust was confirmatory evidence that the anchors had dropped. Bergman waited. If the anchors had been damaged when *U-885's* stem had cut into *Needlefish's* hull, the U-boat would continue on its merry way and grind to a screeching halt on the sharp-toothed coral. Once again, the decision had been made and he was committed. There was no way out. A submarine's diesel engines had no reverse drive to the propellers - the reverse gearing was used for charging the batteries and not for driving the boat. And for this reason U-boat commanders normally manoeuvred on their electric motors when surfaced in confined waters.

But during the final approach to Balabac Machine-maat, Venne had made the unwelcome discovery that *U-885's* bottom plates, strained when she rammed *Needlefish*, were leaking seawater into the battery compartment and the motors were immediately disconnected to enable repairs to be carried out. And at that precise moment, Venne and two of the electricians were lying full-length in the cramped bilge keel isolating the damaged cells and rearranging the power cables by the light of emergency torches.

The deafening rattle of the anchor chains running out, exaggerated by the echoing acoustics of the lower hull, made their ears hurt. Zimberg reached forward and banged Venne's shoulder with his screwdriver.

'Better get out, Kurt - we've grounded on a shoal.'

Venne grunted and started work on the corroded terminals of Cell 68. His foot kicked gently against Zimberg's nose as he thrust back.

'Don't wet your pants! And stop poking that bloody screwdriver up my arse - it's only the anchors running out.'

U-885 suddenly stopped drifting as the anchor chains dragged taut and satisfied that he was on holding ground, Bergman ordered Verlag to let go the stem anchor. Then walking to the port side of the bridge, he leaned on his elbows to watch a small white launch burbling out from the wooden pier. The crew was dressed in the unfamiliar khaki drab of the army and the blood-red emblem of the Rising Sun flapped from the stem.

Bottcher and Siess caught the launch skilfully with their boat hooks as it drifted against the bulbous beam tanks of the U-boat and held it steady while Major Kamatsura stepped awkwardly up onto the steel plates of the foredeck casing. The Oberbootsmann saluted smartly and Lauerbach piped him aboard with due, if unnecessary, ceremony.

'You do my garrison an honour,' Kamatsura bowed to Bergman as he arrived on the bridge. He drew his breath in a sharp hiss and Fujita hissed back with the traditional politeness. Bergman returned the bow but decided against the hiss on the grounds that it might unintentionally degenerate into a somewhat ruder and unharmonious sound. He still found many of the old Japanese customs amusing and he experienced an uncharacteristic feeling of superiority as the two little men went through their mutual obsequies.

Major Kamatsura was resplendent in a fresh white uniform liberally ornamented with gold and medals and Fujita, too, was immaculately turned out in the Imperial Navy's Number One dress. Bergman and the rest of his crew looked more like pirates. Few of them had shaved since leaving Penang and even fewer had washed. Most of the men were wearing only grubby cotton shorts that had once been white although Bergman at least had made some attempt to dress for the occasion by putting on his uniform cap - the gold on which was tarnished green by salt spray - and an almost clean shirt.

'The Commander informs me you have prisoners?' Kamatsura's voice was high-pitched and his English had a strangely sing-song accent which Fujita had managed to discard during his years in America. Bergman nodded.

'Correct, Herr Major. One officer and four enlisted men. Two of the men need urgent medical treatment and Fujita tells me you have a military hospital on Balabac.'

Kamatsura's eyebrows lifted but his impassive face gave no indication of his thoughts. He hissed and bowed.

Bergman took the politeness to be an affirmative answer to his question and he turned to the Ober-bootsmann.

'Bring the prisoners on deck, Kosch.'

Lieutenant Commander Satterlee headed the group as Verlag and Thyssen escorted them up through the lower conning-tower hatch. Hoyt hovered in attendance as Willi Hartmann and another seaman carried the seriously wounded American to the waiting launch and laid him gently on the floor. The other prisoners followed but Satterlee paused and looked up at Bergman.

'Thank you for the excellent treatment you have afforded my men and myself while we have been aboard your boat, Kapitanleutnant. You seem to be a man of honour. I can therefore only believe that you are totally ignorant of the way the Japanese treat their prisoners. And for the sake of your conscience, I hope you will never learn the truth.'

Bergman acknowledged Satterlee's salute with cold correctness. While he dismissed most of the American's accusations as no more than the product of enemy propaganda, he had seen enough in Germany and Occupied Europe to realise that vile things were being done in the name of the Third Reich and its Allies - things that had no point nor purpose and which were committed solely for the sadistic gratification of the perpetrators.

And although, like most Germans, he knew nothing of the horrors of the gas chambers or the Final Solution, Bergman had bitter personal experience of the sufferings of the Jewish people under Hitler. The Gestapo's treatment of Rahel Yousoff, the only woman he had ever loved, had finally opened his eyes to the rottenness of the Nazi apple. And despite his loyalty to his country, he had become an avowed enemy of the mad clique of men who were riding his beloved Germany to destruction.

His thoughts were broken by Kamatsura's polite hiss of farewell. The Japanese army officer bowed low. 'I wish you a pleasant voyage to Nippon, Kapitanleutnant.'

Bergman did not return the bow. 'Thank you, Major. I will pass the names of the prisoners over to the International Red Cross when I get to Tokyo.'

It was meant as a veiled warning but Kamatsura only smiled blandly, bowed once more, and climbed down the ladder to the waiting launch.

'Can you spare a minute, sir?'

Chief Engineer Badenholdt hauled himself up out of the hatch. He looked hot and tired and was wiping oil from his arms with a swab of cotton waste. Bergman forced himself to forget about the prisoners.

'Yes, Chief ?'

'It's that leak in the forward keel section, sir. We've traced it to the starboard bow plates. The water's leaking in badly. Not enough to sink us but there's a danger of the salt contaminating the forward batteries. And you know what that means.'

Bergman knew exactly what it meant. If seawater came into contact with the acid in the batteries, the chemical reaction produced chlorine gas. That was how his father had died in 1918 when the old *UC-115* had been gunned down by a Q-ship off the Flanders coast. It was probably the disaster which U-boat men feared most of all.

'Can you fix it?'

Badenholdt leaned against the side of the bridge, pulled a cigarette out of his pocket and lit it. 'We've two alternatives, sir,' he explained, blowing a plume of blue smoke through his nostrils. 'I can seal off the forward battery compartment so that the gas cannot penetrate into the boat but it would mean a one-third loss of electric power and reduced submerged running-time. Or, if I could lay my hands on some welding equipment, my lads could repair the damaged plates.'

'Time required?'

'Not more than twelve hours. Provided we can get hold of the welding gear.'

Bergman glanced at his watch. Two hours to sundown. They could work by electric light during the dark hours if necessary. And that meant they could still be well away from Balabac by noon. The margin was small but it would just be sufficient. He turned to Fujita.

'Are your army friends likely to have any welding gear we can borrow?'

'I imagine so. A construction battalion is building an airstrip on the eastern side of the island.'

The Kapitanleutnant picked up the six-inch signalling lamp and handed it to the Commander. 'Call up the shore guards and ask the Major to send some equipment out in the launch. And tell him it's urgent. We must be away from here within fifteen hours.'

FOR THE FIRST time in nearly eight weeks, Bergman enjoyed a good night's sleep and he awoke to the appetising aroma of fried eggs wafting into the wardroom from the galley. Fujita was already awake and dressed. He was standing in front of the bronze casket apparently deep in prayer; Bergman slipped out of his bunk quietly so that he was not disturbed. The Japanese officer ended his meditation by kneeling on the deck and touching his forehead to the floor three times. Then, after a short pause, he stood up and greeted the Kapitanleutnant with a broad grin.

'Good morning, Konrad. You're looking better for a good sleep.'

'I feel better, Mitsuru. I don't think I've enjoyed an undisturbed night since we left Lorient in February.'

Fujita sat down at the wardroom table and sipped his fruit juice slowly. He glanced sideways at *U-885*'s skipper curiously.

'Why the rush to get away from here?' he asked. 'Time is your own surely?'

Bergman took a deep mouthful of scalding coffee and swallowed it with obvious satisfaction. He shrugged. 'I must make my rendezvous with the escorting forces off Yakuno Island on time. I don't see the point of steaming ten thousand miles just to get myself sunk by the Imperial Japanese Navy.'

Fujita nodded and returned to his fruit juice. He knew Bergman was lying. The final rendezvous arrangements would be made by radio - no one could expect an accurate landfall after a voyage of eight weeks. He wondered idly what his companion was hiding.

Badenholdt's arrival in the wardroom prevented further speculation.

'Repairs completed, sir,' he informed Bergman. 'Hope there's time for me to grab some breakfast.'

'Take a seat, Chief. And congratulations.' Bergman glanced at his wristwatch. 'I shall be casting off at ten o'clock so as soon as you've had breakfast, you and your lads can have a quick swim in the lagoon. I reckon you all deserve it.' He paused as Klaver, the wardroom steward, brought their breakfast in from the galley. 'Is all the welding gear packed ready to be taken ashore?'

'Yes, sir. Zimberg has stacked it against the deck gun and Hartmann is on guard duty.'

Bergman leaned to one side and lifted the telephone

to the control room. Von Schroeder answered as Duty Officer.

'Get the welding gear on board the launch, Number One. I'll be down in a few minutes. And get four of the lads into uniform as my escort.'

'You are going ashore?' Fujita sounded surprised and more than a little curious.

'Of course. I must thank Major Kamatsura for his assistance. The German Navy still observes the traditional courtesies - and I've got a couple of hours in hand before we sail.'

'But it really is not necessary, Konrad.'

Bergman smiled with unaccustomed sweetness and patted Fujita's arm to soothe his agitation. He knew why he was going ashore. And he suspected this was the reason for his companion's consternation.

'You can come too, Mitsuru,' he said placatingly. 'I shall probably need an interpreter anyway.' Pushing his empty plate to one side he stood up. 'I'll see you on deck in five minutes but first of all I must have a quick wash and put on a decent uniform. Can't have our honourable allies thinking we always go around like unkempt monkeys.'

He disappeared into his tiny cabin on the forward side of the wardroom before Fujita could raise any further objections.

Major Kamatsura looked suitably impressed as Kapitanleutnant Bergman stepped out of the launch and walked down the wooden pier to greet him. His hiss of welcome was a shade more sibilant than usual and his bow several inches more deferential. Bergman's immaculate blue uniform looked almost colourful in contrast to the olive-drab of the army battledress and the insignia of the Knight's Cross of the Iron Cross glinted in the sunlight. He saluted and stood to one side as Oberbootsmann Kosch marched the landing party smartly forward with the welding gear.

A sudden burst of machine-gun fire shattered the still morning air and the birds nestling in the trees wheeled angrily into the sky, screeching shrill protests at the disturbance. Bergman glanced up with narrowed eyes. But he made no comment.

Kamatsura looked uncomfortable. He ran a finger under his collar and exchanged glances with Fujita standing just behind U-885's skipper.

'I appreciate gesture,' the Major bowed. 'But you are anxious to sail away now.'

'Not especially,' Bergman observed slowly. There was an ominous silence brooding over the island in the aftermath of the gunfire and for some strange reason he could feel the short hairs rising on the back of his neck. He could smell death and he was curious to know more.

'Perhaps I could have a word with the American prisoners before I leave,' he added quietly. 'I forgot to make a note of their identity numbers and I shall need them for my report to the Red Cross.'

'Deeply regret request impossible, Kapitan.' Kamatsura bowed eagerly as if to bring the confrontation to a close. 'Now you go back to boat, please.'

Bergman turned to Fujita. 'Tell the Major as forcibly as possible that I intend to see the prisoners. If I knew how to swear in Japanese, I'd tell him myself.'

The Commander looked unhappy. Turning to the army officer, he began speaking rapidly. As far as Bergman could judge from the expression on Kamatsura's face, Fujita was using all the appropriate words. The

Major's lips twisted into a half-snarl as he replied. And as Fujita translated his answer, he stood facing the German U-boat commander with his legs arrogantly braced apart and his right hand grasping the hilt of his sword.

'Major Kamatsura regrets that he cannot comply with your requests,' Mitsuru translated. 'The American prisoners were shot a few moments ago while trying to escape.'

Bergman wasted no more time on the politenesses of the parley. Thrusting Kamatsura aside, he strode down the path leading to the army camp and snapped a sharp order to Kosch for the landing party to follow. The sailors looked slightly bewildered. Hartmann wondered what the hell was going on but he could see that the Old Man was in one hell of a temper.

The Japanese sentries guarding the entrance to the camp jumped to attention and saluted as *U-885's* landing party came into view. Bergman was leading them at a crisp marching pace and the diminutive Major was half-running in the rear to keep up with them. They continued past a line of wooden barrack huts and into a small clearing where a large Japanese flag fluttered life-lessly from the peak of a sturdy pole. A section of six soldiers were standing in line with submachine guns tucked under their arms waiting for the order to dismiss. The NCO in charge gaped toothily as Bergman strode up to him. The Kapitanleutnant ignored the sergeant's salute and nodded towards the four bodies lying twisted and face-up in the long grass.

'The prisoners?'

Fujita translated and the NCO licked his lips unhappily as he nodded. Bergman walked across to the nearest body and rolled it over with the toe of his shoe. He stared down at the wire securing Arnold Knevet's wrists tightly together behind his back.

'Shot while trying to escape?' His voice was ominously quiet as he turned to Kamatsura. 'All four men - in a neat straight line - and your murder squad conveniently drawn up ready. You're a disgrace to the human race, Major.' He swung angrily at Fujita. 'And translate that word for word, Commander!'

'No need, Kapitan,' Kamatsura retorted. 'Words understood perfectly. But honourable Kapitan is wrong. Americans had surrendered. They had no honour. Code of Bushido says execution not murder when man has no honour.'

'I don't give a damn for your bloody code, Major! I demand the immediate return of Lieutenant Commander Satterlee to my custody.'

'Regret impossible, Kapitan. But he will die with honour - Japanese officers grant fellow officers full honour even in death.' Before Bergman could sting out a reply, he heard the tramp of marching feet to his right and swinging around sharply, he saw Satterlee being escorted into the clearing by a squad of armed soldiers with fixed bayonets. The American's face was bruised and bloody and he was limping awkwardly with his arms pinioned together behind his back.

'Execution party - *halt!*'

Lieutenant Yatsumichi slipped on a pair of white gloves and waited as Satterlee was prodded forward clear of the escort. 'The prisoner will kneel.'

Satterlee seemed to know what to expect. He dropped obediently to his knees and turned his head towards *U-885*'s captain.

'I reckon I had you figured wrong, Herr Kapitanleutnant,' he said bitterly. 'I see they've found you a ringside seat for the entertainment. I hope you rot in hell!'

He spat at Bergman's feet as the Japanese NCO seized him by the hair and forced him to bow his head. Lieutenant Yatsumichi smoothed his gloves carefully, took up a position on the prisoner's left-hand side, and slowly unsheathed his sword. The sharp steel blade glinted in the morning sun as he raised it high above his head, clasping the handle with both hands.

Bergman stood rooted to the ground petrified with shock. It was utterly unbelievable and for a few moments his brain was unable to assimilate the enormity of the atrocity he was about to witness. Kosch, too, froze with horror as Yatsumichi raised the sword. Every instinct urged him to leap forward and tear the weapon from the Japanese officer's immaculately-gloved hands but the iron bounds of discipline restrained the impulse. He knew that the skipper would not permit this hideous thing to happen and he waited confidently for the Kapitanleutnant's order.

But no order came. For the first time in his life, Bergman found himself facing an evil that was totally beyond his comprehension or experience. And paralysed by the obscene barbarity, his brain refused to react.

There was a sickening thud as the razor-edged sword sliced down and Willi Hartmann's eyes flickered whitely as he fainted on the grass. Kosch had sufficient sense to shut his eyes at the last moment but it required a strong effort of will to open them again. Only Bergman faced it out and, standing rigidly to attention, he showed no emotion of any kind as Yatsumichi's execution sword flashed down.

Satterlee's body fell forward onto the grass as a fountain

of blood splattered from the arteries of the severed neck. The head rolled grotesquely towards Bergman and came to rest at his feet. The eyes were still open and they stared accusingly up at the man who had handed him over to his murderers.

Bergman's face was drained of expression as he stared down at the hideous object lying bleeding at his feet. He remained motionless for a few moments, his head bowed as if in prayer. Then he stooped and gently closed Satterlee's eyelids.

'Try to make allowances - it is not easy for a Westerner to understand our customs,' Fujita urged quietly. 'In the Orient, we see life and death in a different way.'

He flinched away as he read the cold hate in the Kapitanleutnant's eyes. There was nothing he could do, nothing he could say to bridge the gap that yawned between their cultures.

'Inform Major Kamatsura that he is to accompany me back to *U-885*.' Bergman's voice was as cold and flat as his expressionless eyes. But it still contained the sharp quality of command. 'Tell him I wish to take a drink with him before we leave.'

Fujita was bewildered. It was impossible to guess what was going on inside his companion's brain, yet to extend an invitation to the man responsible for the execution of the American prisoners seemed utterly incredible. He hesitated.

'Go ahead - invite him.'

Fujita bowed politely to the Major and spoke rapidly. Kamatsura seemed equally surprised. He was obviously questioning the unexpected invitation and even Fujita's assurances failed to convince him. He said something in reply and nodded at the Commander's answer. Turning to Bergman, he bowed his acceptance with a sharp indrawn hiss.

No one spoke as the little procession returned to the pier. Kosch and the landing party kept their distance behind the three officers. Hartmann's face was green with shock and he stumbled awkwardly as he struggled to keep up with the others. He desperately wanted to be sick but he was equally determined to restrain his natural impulses while the Japanese were watching. He half fell into the waiting launch and withdrew into the bows as if to keep the contamination of Kamatsura's presence at the maximum distance.

Like Fujita and the other members of the landing party, Willi was initially appalled by the skipper's invitation to the Japanese major. But he had served with Bergman long enough to recognise the expression in his eyes. And he took cold comfort from the fact that everything was not quite as it appeared on the surface. The Old Man was deep - very deep. And in Willi's opinion, he was up to something.

Bergman was solicitous in his attentions to Kamatsura as he helped him out of the launch onto the U-boat's deck. And having seen his guest safely to the wardroom, he returned to the bridge and instructed Fujita to send the launch back to the island.

'Tell them to return to embark the Major when they receive our signal.'

Fujita nodded and shouted instructions to the pilot of the launch. The man held his hand up in acknowledgement and, pushing open the throttles, he swung the boat away from the submarine's side, turned in a wide circle, and steered back to their pier. Fujita watched him depart and then, with a shrug, he left the bridge and made his way down to the wardroom.

Bergman was already pouring a large drink for the Major who, excited by his bizarre surroundings, was staring wide-eyed in every direction. Handing a glass to his guest and passing another to Fujita, the Kapitanleutnant raised his own in a toast.

'To the Emperor,' he began in English. *'Das grossen Schwanz.'*

Von Schroeder looked up sharply as he heard Bergman's obscenity. There must be something going on, he thought to himself. Or perhaps the Old Man's already had a skinful ashore.

Kamatsura smiled pompously and acknowledging the toast with a bow, he swallowed the drink.

'And to your great leader - Adolf Hitler,' he responded.

Bergman raised his glass. *'Mein arsch!'* he bowed.

Von Schroeder turned his head away to hide his laughter as the two Japanese officers solemnly clinked their glasses and chorused, *'Mein arsch* - Adolf Hitler.'

Bergman produced another bottle of Highland Glen and refilled his guest's glass to the brim. The Major blinked myopically and nodded his thanks. The whisky was neat and strong and his head was beginning to swim.

'Are we ready for sea, Number One?' The Kapitanleutnant asked the question in German in the safe knowledge that Kamatsura would not understand.

'Yes, sir.'

'Very good - raise anchor and go out astern. Steer zero-two-five once we are clear of the reefs. Remain surfaced in Condition One alert.'

'Do I call up the launch, sir?'

Bergman shook his head. 'No - I intend our little fat friend to enjoy a trip at the expense of the Third Reich.'

Von Schroeder saluted, bowed to the two Japanese Officers, and slipped through the curtains into the control room.

Fujita looked up suddenly as he heard the departure orders being shouted and he glanced curiously at Bergman as the electric motors began to whine. What the devil was going on? On reflection, he decided not to ask. Better to wait to see, in view of the circumstances. Kamatsura seemed blissfully unaware of the sudden activity inside the U-boat. His belly glowed warmly from the whisky and everything had a roseate glow. In his own mind, he had scored a moral victory over the German captain and he saw no reason for refusing the fruits of his success. It was surprising how quickly Europeans found a new respect for the Japanese Empire when they saw evidence of its power.

He smiled broadly as Bergman refilled the empty glass and he assumed the gentle rocking motion of the U-boat to be no more than a warning that he was drinking too much. Strange that Fujita should be so quiet, he thought to himself. But it was typical of these damned Navy snobs. All airs and graces and then sulking because the Army is given the place of honour.

Fujita heard the sharp 'ting' of the engine-room telegraph and he fidgeted uncomfortably on his chair as U-885 edged stem-first out of the lagoon. His loyalty to Japan struggled with his contempt for the despicable murderer the Kapitanleutnant had chosen to entertain. And for the second time that morning, he decided to wait and see.

Having checked that his guest had a full glass,

Bergman lifted the telephone to the control room. 'Report, please.'

'We're standing well clear of the entrance, sir,' von Schroeder told him. 'Turning in thirty seconds to pick up course as ordered.'

'Any response from the shore yet?'

'None, sir. The launch is still tied up to the jetty. They don't seem able to make up their minds about what we're doing.'

'Well, they've left it too late to catch us now, Number One. Turn over to main engines and ring for maximum speed.'

Kamatsura looked up in surprise at the sudden belching roar of the main engines. *U-885* rolled violently as the propellers bit into the water and his mouth dropped open in astonishment. He jabbered something to Fujita but Bergman did not wait for a translation.

'Tell him we're running an engine test,' he informed the Japanese Commander. 'And then you get topside and take over the Watch.'

Fujita said something to the Major and Bergman waited tensely to see Kamatsura's reaction. Although he instinctively trusted his companion, his old caution made him wary of treachery from even his most loyal friends. But Kamatsura merely smiled and nodded as Fujita reassured him and picking up his glass, he drained it dry with a flourish.

Mitsuru hesitated for a moment as if to speak. Then thinking better of it, he ducked through the curtains and disappeared into the control room. Whatever the Kapitanleutnant planned to do it was better, he reasoned, that he did it alone and without witnesses.

Bergman waited for a few moments as he weighed his

final decision. Then, without hesitation, he moved across to one of the lockers, reached inside, and lifted out a revolver. His eyes were cold and hard as he turned to face Kamatsura.

'You referred to the Code of the Bushido earlier today, Herr Major, when you offered it as an excuse for your actions against the prisoners. Well, the German Navy also has a code of conduct. And as Captain of this U-boat, I am empowered to carry out summary execution for certain prescribed offences. One of those offences is cold-blooded, willful murder.'

Kamatsura was still rising from the chair as Bergman's bullet smashed into his chest at point-blank range. The force of the impact threw him backwards against the starboard bulkhead. His bulging eyes opened wide in surprise and his mouth opened to speak. But the sound never fought its way past the death rattle clogging his throat. Pitching forward to die, he lay completely still.

Bergman threw the gun down on the table and pushed his way through the curtains. He met von Schroeder hurrying down the narrow companionway towards the sound of the pistol shot.

'I am afraid our guest has met with a slight accident,' Bergman told him calmly. 'Pipe some hands to get him on deck.' Offering nothing further by way of explanation, the Kapitanleutnant continued into the control room and climbed the ladder leading to the bridge. Fujita was watching the horizon through his binoculars and he turned as Bergman hoisted himself up through the hatchway. Although the sharp crack of the pistol shot had been muffled by the stout steel of the hull, the Japanese officer had no doubts in his mind as to what he had heard and his slant eyes narrowed as he watched U-885's captain.

Bergman walked to the side of the bridge, stared out over the empty sea for a few seconds, and breathed the salt air deep into his lungs as if cleansing his body. His eyes were clear and untroubled as he turned to face Fujita.

'Major Kamatsura is dead. He shot himself - what do you call it? *hari kari?*'

It was impossible to read Fujita's thoughts. His eyes glowed like deep black pools and he made an odd clicking sound with his tongue. 'Suicide,' he observed impassively. 'It is an honourable way to die in the circumstances.'

Bergman nodded. He did not know whether he could still trust his companion but it was one more chance he had to take. And it was essential to cover his tracks now that the deed was done. He had only killed a man once before in his life - the coxswain of *UB-44*, Herzog. And that had been easy. No one had doubted that he'd been drowned with the rest of the crew when the U-boat had sunk. But that was different.

The garrison on Balabac Island knew that Kamatsura had gone on board *U-885* at the Kapitanleutnant's invitation. And, equally, they knew he had not returned. He realised, too, that the execution of the American prisoners must by now be common knowledge amongst the crew. His men were not fools and they had probably guessed the truth already. And, of course, that included Fujita.

'We must inform the authorities,' Bergman said slowly. 'If I dictate a signal, will you translate it for Gamheim to transmit?'

'Of course.'

Bergman tried to read Fujita's eyes but it was impossible. He gave about as much away of his secret thoughts as a Hamburg whore entertaining an over-enthusiastic client. He mentally shrugged away his doubts. He was sure he could trust the Commander. But even if he couldn't and if Fujita fed another message into the proposed signal, there was nothing he could do about it. He had taken his decision, acted upon it, and now he must face the consequences.

A scuffling noise from the hatch interrupted his thoughts as he began composing the signal. And he could identify Hartmann's voice amongst the commotion.

'Go careful, Max. Don't drop the little yellow bastard.'

'Well, lift his bloody legs up then.'

Bottcher's florid face suddenly emerged from the hatch. He moved awkwardly under the weight of his burden, eased his buttocks over the lip of the opening, and slowly eased Kamatsura's legs onto the deck of the bridge.

Bergman tactfully led Fujita over to the shade of the starboard side so that he was screened from the sweating efforts of the amateur pallbearers and began dictating his message.

'From CO *U*-885 to Base Commander Balabac Island. Regret to inform you that Major Kamatsura committed suicide at...' he glanced down at his watch, '... 11:25 this morning. He will be buried at sea with full military honours.'

He waited until Fujita had finished taking down the signal. He nodded his approval as it was read back.

'Good - now get that translated and transmitted as soon as possible. And tell Gamheim to repeat it to Combined Fleet HQ at Tokyo.'

Fujita acknowledged the order and turned towards the conning-tower hatch. Kamatsura's body was now stretched out on the deck and as he passed, the little Commander bowed his respects to the corpse.

Bergman waited until Fujita was safely out of earshot before issuing his instructions for the disposal of his late and unlamented guest. They were both simple and unequivocal.

'Sling the bastard over the side!'

'What about the full military honours, sir?' von Schroeder inquired with a grin.

'Tell the burial party to take their caps off - and they can whistle the Jap national anthem if they know it.'

Hartmann and Bottcher took their cue with unexpected alacrity. Moving fore and aft of the body, they seized the Major's legs and arms and lifted him up like a sack of potatoes. The body, carefully weighted with iron bars, struck the water with a loud splash and vanished into the black depths beneath the surface.

'And I hope he don't poison the bloody fish,' Willi spat by way of an epitaph.

'Take over the Watch, Number One!'

Von Schroeder acknowledged the order with a salute and moved across to the centre of the bridge where he could see the gyro repeater. 'What orders, sir?'

'Reduce to half-speed and steer zero-four-five. You should sight a junk at thirteen-hundred hours bearing northeasterly. If you don't, I want you to circle and wait. It will be wearing a length of red silk along its stem quarter. Call me as soon as you spot it.'

The Executive Officer nodded and settled comfortably at his station. There were times when he wished the skipper wasn't so damned secretive. He wondered idly what the mysterious junk was doing and what Bergman was up to now. But at least it solved the other puzzle of why the skipper was so anxious to get away from Balabac within a predetermined period. There was one consolation, however. It showed that every move they made had been carefully planned in advance. And it was a reassuring thought when one was 10,000 miles from home.

Bergman stuck his head inside Gamheim's cramped little radio cabin and nodded to Fujita. 'Signal transmitted?'

'Yes - Gamheim has just received an acknowledgement from Balabac.'

'Any problems?'

'No. In fact, they didn't seem at all surprised.' For the first time since the executions, Fujita grinned. 'I gather that the Major was none too popular with his own men either.'

Bergman read his own interpretation into Fujita's remark with a sense of relief. But he gave no outward indication of his feelings. He turned to Gamheim.

'I want you to start transmitting the letters QQ at thirty second intervals on 4995 kc/s. As soon as you receive an acknowledgement, you can switch on our homing beacon.'

'Very good, sir. Letters QQ, thirty seconds, 4995 band. I will start transmission immediately.'

Fujita said nothing until they were out of the radio cabin and in the wardroom.

'What's going on now, Konrad?' he asked.

Bergman smiled. 'Nothing very interesting I'm afraid, Mitsuru. Only a refueling operation. I have a rendezvous with a trading junk carrying one hundred barrels of fuel oil.' He saw the astonishment on Fujita's face and laughed. 'You seem to have forgotten that this part of the world used to be in the German Empire before the Great

War. A lot of our people stayed on afterwards. So when we decided to build up secret fuel dumps for our surface raiders in 1935, we had a ready-made organization to work with. Doenitz arranged a series of emergency refueling points before we left Lorient and this is our second rendezvous; we picked up another supply earlier off the Chagos Archipelago while we were crossing the Indian Ocean. And in another hour or so, we'll be topping up our bunkers for a further fourteen days or so.'

Fujita nodded. He said nothing but it was difficult to hide the gleam of admiration in his eyes - if only the Japanese Navy had known about these secret fuel dumps. The Germans seemed to leave nothing to chance. And while the Japanese Navy was restricting operations because of oil shortages, Germany's carefully prepared contingency planning could still feed the hungry engines of a lone sea wolf 10,000 miles away from home.

Suddenly, for the first time, he realised that his presence on board *U-885* was entirely superfluous. Bergman was quite capable of reaching Japan without his assistance. And the Kapitanleutnant seemed equal to any challenge or emergency he found facing him. There was something almost inhuman about Bergman's casual omnipotence and it made him feel uncomfortable and inadequate.

And yet, if *U-885*'s captain was telling the truth, there was one chink in his armour of apparent invincibility.

Someone in Germany wanted him dead.

Fujita shook his head sorrowfully as he realised that he would never really understand the European way of doing things.

SEVEN

The bustling, purposeful atmosphere of Sasebo, Japan's great naval base on the western coast of her most southerly island, Kyushu, came like a breath of fresh salt air to Bergman's nostrils after the stuffy formalities of Tokyo. And as *U-885* picked her way carefully through the tangled mass of warships gathered in the vast land-locked bay, the war seemed suddenly closer and more urgent once again.

Bergman was not surprised by the failure of his mission to the Japanese capital. He had always considered Doenitz too optimistic about his chances and he had dismissed Kommodore Schiller's alternative long before his arrival in Tokyo Bay. After the Penang incident, he had no intention of setting himself up as a sitting target for the *Kempei Tai* by attempting to steal Japan's greatest military secret. And he was still nervously waiting for a reaction to Major Kamatsura's suicide.

The senior naval officers in Tokyo had greeted him with a marked lack of warmth and for ten days Bergman found himself being shifted from one department to another as each admiral sought to avoid answering awkward questions. His biggest disappointment was his failure to meet the legendary Yamamoto, the admiral who had achieved worldwide fame for the attack on Pearl Harbor. But the war was moving too fast and Japan's naval C-in-C had already left for Truk to discuss plans for avenging the defeats of the Guadalcanal campaign.

The German radar equipment, however, proved a great attraction and Bergman spent hours demonstrating and explaining it to his many visitors. *U-885*, too, created considerable interest and there was a steady stream of senior submarine officers anxious to inspect its technical secrets.

From a Japanese point of view, the visit was a resounding success but despite their avariciousness in acquiring Germany's scientific know-how, the Japanese showed a strange reluctance to reveal their own. He was allowed, after much pressure, to see a *Type-93* torpedo performing in the Inland Sea during destroyer exercises but that was as close as he was permitted to get and he wondered bitterly whether the Japanese Admiralty realised that the Kriegsmarine was its ally.

Although irritated by the bland refusals he received, it was little more than he had expected and after his chat with Fujita the previous week, Bergman had already decided in his own mind that the oxygen-propelled torpedo was of no practical value to Germany due to its large size.

What had struck him though was the extraordinary rivalry that existed between the Japanese army and the Imperial Navy - a rivalry that had by that time reached ludicrous lengths. The Kriegsmarine's power struggle with Goering's Luftwaffe had always been a bone of contention with German naval officers but by comparison with Japanese inter-service rivalry, the two services might have been blood brothers.

Sighting a submarine moving south through the Bungo Channel, he was disconcerted to learn from Fujita that it was an army submarine specially designed for troop and supply transportation and manned entirely by army personnel. Further probing on Bergman's part when he arrived in Tokyo revealed that the army also built and operated its own cargo ships while the Navy maintained a complete motor transport corps for use ashore. There were even three separate weather observation organisations - each jealously guarding its data and forecasts from the other - run by the Navy, the Army, and a civil authority.

It was an organisational nightmare which no one in Europe had ever suspected and Bergman knew that his intelligence report on the subject would probably be of more value to Germany's strategic planners than a dozen detailed drawings of naval secrets. Fujita, strutting proudly like a small boy showing off his toys, was unaware of the Kapitanleutnant's interest. Complacently convinced that Bergman was impressed by the outward display of Japanese war strength, he little realised that the German officer's probing and seemingly pointless inquiries were revealing Japan's vaunted military superiority for what it really was - a colossal sham.

'Object fine on port bow, sir!'

The keen-eyed Siess had spotted something small and low in the water. It was moving at an angle away from the U-boat but Bergman had it focused in his glasses within seconds.

'Slow ahead both - half left rudder.'

'Group down - slow ahead both.'

Bergman's first reaction was one of anticlimax. The black slug-like object was running awash and as the U-boat turned, it slipped beneath the surface in a flurry of spray. Within moments, it had completely vanished from sight and only the swirling disturbance on the top of the water remained to show that something had been there.

'What did you make of it, Konrad?'

Bergman half-turned to find Fujita standing at his side with his binoculars trained on the place where the thing had disappeared.

'Resume course, Steuermann - half-speed ahead.' He waited until *U-885* had completed her course correction before turning his attention to the question. He shrugged. 'Could have been a dolphin playing on the surface or a fish of some sort.'

'Sure?'

Bergman hesitated. To be honest, he was not sure. He had caught only a quick glimpse of the submerging object but it had left him with the distinct impression that it was both manmade and under human control. He laughed.

'All right, Mitsuru, I know you're dying to tell me. What is it? Your new secret weapon?'

Fujita smiled mysteriously. He looked complacently satisfied that Bergman, for once, had exposed a gap in his omnipotence.

'It was a midget submarine.'

'Rubbish!' Bergman dismissed the explanation out of hand. 'I've read a great deal about your midget submarines; in fact, it's a branch of underwater warfare that interests me a great deal. The *Type-A* midgets you operated against Pearl Harbor were near enough eighty feet long. And from what I've seen in the Intelligence reports at U-boat HQ, the British midgets are over fifty feet. Apart from which it was going too bloody fast.' He called across to Siess standing lookout on the forecasing. 'You had that object in sight long enough to judge its speed, Hans. What did you make it?'

'Twenty-five to thirty knots, sir.'

'I thought so,' Bergman beamed triumphantly. 'And there's no submarine afloat, let alone a midget, that can travel more than twenty knots. Now pull the other one.'

Fujita was still smiling as if enjoying a secret joke. 'You will see, Konrad, you will see. Take my word for it. It was a midget submarine although, to be more precise, perhaps I should describe it as a human torpedo.'

For the first time since Admiral Doenitz had briefed him for his Far East mission, Bergman's interest was aroused. To hell with a torpedo that was too big to be used by the U-boats - this was much more important. Sometime in the course of the next year, the Allies would have to invade Europe if they wanted to set up a Second Front and overthrow the Nazi regime. And operating in the narrow shoaling waters of the North Sea and Channel coasts, hundreds of miniature submarines capable of mass production on a large scale could be the very weapon the Kriegsmarine needed to counter the invasion threat.

'There's no time to fill you in on the details,' Fujita told him. 'We'll be entering the inner harbour inside ten minutes and you'll need all your attention for getting U-885 berthed. But I'll take you along to meet Captain Sendai tomorrow. He was a classmate of mine at Etajima so it will be easy to arrange. And you can see a *Kaiten* with your own eyes.'

Bergman accepted the invitation with a casual nod that carefully concealed his excitement. If the *Kaiten* was all that Fujita said it was, he had found a weapon that could win the war for Germany. Suddenly and without warning, U-885's tedious and apparently useless mission to Japan promised to be the most rewarding voyage since Columbus had set sail to discover the New World.

CAPTAIN HOCHIRO SENDAI proved to be a happy contrast to the blandly unhelpful admirals Bergman had encountered in Tokyo. Despite his lack of height, he was a bull of a man with a broad pockmarked face, heavy shoulders, and the build of a Sumo wrestler. Unlike the majority of senior officers in the Imperial Navy, he disdained the immaculate uniform of the quarterdeck and when he came out to greet the U-boat commander, he was wearing a disreputable oil-stained overall from which all insignia of rank had long since disappeared. Only his blue uniform cap with the row of gold oak leaves on its peak indicated that he was a post-captain and even that had seen better days.

Submarine Experimental Division 14 was situated two miles up a stagnant creek north of the main dockyard. It was guarded by a high wooden fence and armed sentries ensured that no unauthorised persons passed beyond its heavily-barred gates. Inside, and in contrast to the dank rotting vegetation that surrounded the creek, everything was spick-and-span and shipshape. Sendai's headquarters were situated in a low stone-built office adjacent to the jetty and a series of prefabricated corrugated iron huts housed the machinery and workshops.

Sendai had made a study of the German U-boat war and he was already familiar with Bergman's reputation.

And having spent several years as an Assistant Naval Attache in Berlin, his command of German was passably good.

After his experience on Balabac Island, Bergman had developed a tendency to regard all Japanese as barbarians - an opinion that had hardened during his brief visit to Tokyo when he had found the rigid formalities of Japanese etiquette as antagonising as the harsh brutality of the combat officers. But Sendai, like Fujita, was a no-nonsense sensible human being and he quickly developed a liking for the thick-set little Captain who chattered away in a strange German dialect liberally spattered with obsolete slang expressions dating back to the early thirties.

But despite a genuine interest, Bergman found the relentless monologue a trifle wearing. His head was still throbbing from his first night ashore in Sasebo with Fujita and what he really needed was somewhere cool and quiet to rest and a long cold drink to wash the sourness from his mouth. Not that he had any complaints about Mitsuru's hospitality. It was simply that he was not used to a non-stop intake of *sake* or to the delights of being bathed and massaged by two skilful *geishas* at four o'clock in the morning.

His body still throbbed sensually from the remem-bered caress of their butterfly hands on his naked flesh and apart from the aching pain in his head, he felt remark-ably refreshed despite a demanding and almost sleepless night.

Sendai guided him down to the wooden jetty and, still talking volubly, led him along the narrow catwalk to a small basin located on the left-hand side of the creek. It was screened from sight by tall clumps of bamboo and

Bergman's eyes suddenly gleamed as he saw the slim tubular object lying in the water.

'This is a *Kaiten Type-i*,' the Captain explained proudly. 'Of course we are now developing an improved version but I think you will still find much of interest in this prototype.'

The *Kaiten* was just under fifty feet in length and it looked like a cross between a torpedo and a miniature submarine. The stem section, with its diving rudders and twin contra-rotating propellers, was pure torpedo but a tiny periscope amidships indicated that it had a human pilot while the bow section's outer casing and flooding holes was that of a small submarine.

'Which is it?' he asked. 'A torpedo or a submarine?'

Sendai laughed. 'I suppose you could say both, Kapitanleutnant. Basically it is a *Type-93* torpedo modified to take a one-man crew. The warhead is fitted into the bows in conventional fashion and the pilot steers it at the target, locks it on course, and then escapes through a hatch in the hull.'

Bergman crouched down to examine the details of the strange little craft. It was certainly a fascinating concept although he had certain reservations about the pilot escaping.

'What's it powered by?' he asked. 'I saw one in the harbour yesterday and it seemed to be travelling at least thirty knots.'

'We used the standard *Type-93* engine initially,' Sendai explained. 'As you know, this is an oxygen-enriched unit and the *Kaiten* version gave us about thirty knots. But this little baby has just arrived from the Mitsubishi works at Yokohama. It's the latest design and is fitted with a hydrogen-peroxide engine with a power output of around eighteen hundred horsepower. It can make forty knots under combat conditions and it has a cruising range of fifty miles. Just imagine the effect of a torpedo with that sort of range and under the control of a human brain.'

During his stint at U-boat headquarters Bergman had heard numerous rumours about Professor Walter's experiments with hydrogen-peroxide power units and it was common knowledge that Doenitz was planning a revolutionary U-boat design based on these new engines. He knew also that Walter's experimental work had been beset by continual problems and that the construction programme was suffering serious delays in consequence. And yet, unknown to Germany's scientists, the Japanese had perfected a workable engine based on the same principle.

This was the real Tokyo Torpedo - the proverbial crock of gold at the end of the rainbow. And as he stood staring at the grey cylinder floating gently in the yellow muddy water of the Heiso Creek, Bergman knew he must have it. Somehow he had to get a *Kaiten* back to Germany so that Walter's experts could examine it and perfect their own engine for the new *Type XXI* U-boat.

'I've never seen anything like it, Captain,' he told Sendai truthfully and the little Japanese officer visibly swelled with pride as he heard the note of undisguised admiration in the Kapitanleutnant's voice.

'If you'd like to come along with me, I have one of the new *Kaitens* stripped down in Number Four Workshop,' he offered eagerly. 'You can see all the details for yourself and my staff will be happy to answer any questions you might have.'

'You can tell me one thing right now,' Bergman told

him. 'How the hell do you launch a thing like this? You must be able to take it to the target or else it's only fit for coastal defence work.'

Sendai pointed to a large *I-class* submarine lying at a buoy in the mouth of the creek. 'Several of our standard cruiser submarines have been equipped with rails and clamps and they are fitted to carry anything up to six *Kaiten* weapons on deck. Launching is carried out at sea when the mother ship approaches within range of the selected target.'

Bergman's agile brain swiftly detected a flaw. Although he was personally impressed by Japan's achievements in the field of midget submarine warfare, his professional submariner's mind could visualise the drawbacks.

'But if you surface to launch the *Kaitens*, you lose the element of surprise,' he pointed out.

'But we don't,' beamed Sendai.

'Then how the hell do you get the pilot into it?'

'Our men are specially trained. They enter the *Kaiten* on the surface several hours before the attack area is reached. They remain inside their weapons until the submarine commander gives the order for their release. They are therefore launched from below the surface in complete privacy.'

Bergman could not repress a grin over Sendai's difficulty in finding the right word in German but he knew what the Captain meant. At the same time, he felt a new admiration for the men who had been trained to pilot the weapon. It took a hell of a lot of guts to sit trapped inside a torpedo for hours on end and riding piggyback on a submerged submarine completely cut off from all means of escape. Germany's scientists would have to come up with a more practical scheme than that before the Kriegs-marine accepted *Kaitens* into service. Doenitz would never order his U-boatmen to face that sort of ordeal.

Sendai kept his promise to show him everything and by the time they left Workshop Four, Bergman's brain was dizzy with facts and figures. Thirty minutes was scarcely long enough to assimilate the plethora of mechanical detail which the Captain made available. They walked slowly down the trim gravel path and stopped outside the door of SUBEXDIV 14's office.

'What are the chances of seeing a *Kaiten* in action?'

'It can be arranged,' Sendai nodded smilingly. 'I-202 is going out on a training exercise after lunch. Perhaps you and Fujita would like to join me.'

Bergman had really made his request more in hope than in anticipation and the Captain's offer, after the off-hand treatment he had received in Tokyo, left him open-mouthed. He stammered his thanks.

'I hope you will let me return the compliment by inviting you for a diving exercise on *U-885*, Captain Senai. Although we have nothing to match your new weapons, I'm sure you will find much of interest.'

Sendai accepted the invitation with alacrity and the mutual bowing and handshaking to seal the deal was finally interrupted by Fujita who pointed out plaintively that he hadn't had a drink since breakfast. Sendai bellowed with laughter and ignoring the wet oil on his overalls, he clapped one arm around the Commander's shoulders and the other around Bergman and escorted them to the mess hut.

Bergman was too excited at the prospect of his coming trip in I-202 to enjoy his lunch and he toyed with the unappetising raw fish while the two Japanese officers reminisced enthusiastically about old times together in the submarine service. Now that he had a chance of acquiring information of value to Germany, he felt suddenly more relaxed and could look at matters more objectively. His visit to Tokyo had been totally without incident and he was beginning to think that the Penang shooting had been no more than a tragic coincidence. Perhaps Fujita's original suggestion that it was only a feud over the services of a *geisha* was right. The fact that the killer was a member of the *Kempei Tai* stretched the arm of coincidence rather far but looking at the situation rationally, Bergman could not see how Gorst or the Gestapo could harm him in the Far East. And as he started to eat his lychees, he concluded that he had been worrying too much ...

By comparison with the sleekly compact U-boats with which Bergman was more familiar, *I*-202 was a veritable marine monster. The old *UB*-44 had been barely 218 feet in length from stem to stern and just 20 feet across at her widest girth. His new boat, *U*-885, was comfortably bigger at 287 feet and 24 feet. But the Type *B-j* to which *I*-202 belonged dwarfed her German sisters into insignificance. She was 336 feet long and was fifty percent wider than *UB*-44 at 30 feet. And that was only the beginning.

The forward section of her conning tower had been extended towards the bows to form an aircraft hanger and she was equipped with a small seaplane for scouting operations. On deck, abaft the conning tower, was a cruiser-sized 5.5″ gun and in addition to two 25mm AA guns, she was fitted with that rare luxury for a Japanese submarine: a *Type*-22 air-warning radar although as Bergman soon discovered, the set was usually out of service due to various technical malfunctions.

Yet despite her enormous size, she was slower than *U-885* both on the surface and submerged and her operational range was four thousand miles less. As Sendai explained during the trip out to the training area west of Hirado, the loss in performance was due mainly to Japan's production problems. The powerful diesels for which it was designed had never left the factory and, like so many other Japanese warships, the submarine had to make do with substitute engines which were too underpowered to meet the demands made upon them.

By German standards, she was a badly-designed boat and in Bergman's eyes, technically ten years behind the times. For one thing, she required a crew of 100 men whereas the scientifically-planned controls of *U-885* enabled the German boat to be fully combat operational with only a 57-man crew. But the thing that surprised him most of all was the monster's puny attack capacity. *U-885*'s six torpedo tubes were backed up by a reserve of 24 weapons. *I-202* had six tubes also but despite her immeasurably greater size, she carried only 18 torpedoes. And that, to Bergman, meant a loss of sinking potential of six ships per patrol.

His careful observations of the Jap submarine's shortcomings were interrupted as Sendai called the *Kaiten* pilots on deck to embark in their weapons. Taking a position at the front of the bridge overlooking the seaplane hangar, Bergman watched intently as the two young officers climbed up special portable ladders to the torpedoes and slid down through the opened hatches. There was no sense of drama or excitement in the occasion and he felt a sense of anticlimax as the routine proceeded.

Here were two men willing to die for their Emperor at the controls of the most fantastic sea weapons ever invented. And yet they were being embarked with as little fuss as he would have expected had they been going for a sail around the bay in a dinghy. Bergman wondered whether a combat launching would be quite so prosaic. Somehow he doubted it.

The deck handling crew clamped the hatch covers and pulled the locking bars into position while a senior Petty Officer carefully checked the chocks and fasteners that held the *Kaitens* to the deck. Then, satisfied that the release equipment was functioning correctly, he shouted the handling party into line and marched them smartly back to the conning tower.

Sendai spoke to each *Kaiten* pilot in turn over the telephone link. Instrument readings were checked, pressure gauges called over, and the compasses were corrected against *I-202's* master gyro.

'The *Kaitens* will be released in one hour thirty minutes precisely. On launching, you are to steer on bearing zero-five-zero and make for base. I shall expect to find you moored to the Main Channel buoy when we return.'

And the best of luck, thought Bergman. Rather you than me. The very thought of being locked inside the tiny submarines was enough to give anyone claustrophobia, even someone as tough as the Kapitanleutnant who had been brought up in U-boats. There was probably no time to worry once the *Kaiten* was running. But it needed a peculiar type of cold-blooded courage to endure that pre-launch period when the midget craft was still firmly secured to the mother ship's deck and there was nothing to do but think.

Pushing the morbid thoughts from his mind, Bergman settled down in a comer of the control room to observe the

Japanese diving routines and aside from the tense moments of the launch itself, he gave no further thought to the two *Kaiten* pilots for the rest of the exercise.

Sendai's expectations, however, proved over-optimistic and when *I-202* nosed her way into the creek on her electric motors, only one of the *Kaitens* was moored against the buoy. *Sho-i* Hyuga, the pilot of *Kaiten* No. 1, was sitting astride his weapon as the submarine stopped engines and drifted towards him. A launch from the base hovered in the background like a mother cat watching its kitten.

'Where is Umikaze?' Sendai shouted from the bridge as soon as Hyuga was within earshot.

'I think his weapon sank five miles after launching, sir. We were running close together and I sighted his periscope several times. I could hear his engine misfiring and he blew tanks to surface. But she must have been flooding fast. That was the last I saw of him.'

Sendai nodded, handed over the berthing to the First Officer, and paced the bridge with his hands clasped behind his back and his massive shoulders hunched despondently.

'I can understand how you feel, sir,' Bergman told him sympathetically. 'I have lost men as well - I know how one blames oneself.'

Sendai made a strange clicking noise with his tongue. 'I am not grieving for Umikaze,' he said softly. 'He has gone to a hero's death. He is at peace. And there are plenty more young men eager to volunteer in his place. My concern is over the loss of a valuable *Kaiten*. We are not yet in full production and the loss of a single *Kaiten* which does not involve the sinking of an enemy ship is a tragedy for Japan.' His eyes were suddenly dark and candid. 'At this moment in our history, ships are of more importance than men.'

Bergman nodded insincerely. That wasn't the way he saw things. And because his men knew it, they trusted him implicitly. He began to wonder whether the development of weapons like the *Kaiten* and the *Kamikaze* suicide bomber was symptomatic of the Japanese disregard for human life.

'We must solve this flooding problem,' Sendai continued as if the death of *Sho-i* Umikaze were of no more consequence than the loss of an unimportant nut and bolt. 'The weapons function perfectly and then, without warning, they start flooding and the pilots seem unable to stabilise the trim. I must go through the drawings again - please excuse me.'

He bowed politely and hurried ashore to continue his search for a solution. Bergman had suddenly ceased to be of any interest to him - all that mattered was the *Kaiten*.

Bergman was still brooding on the incident as the Navy jeep rattled its way to Sasebo an hour later. Sendai had made no effort to locate the sunken *Kaiten* even though he had an approximate fix on its last known position. His lack of concern for the pilot was something that irritated Bergman but the Kapitanleutnant had wisely kept his thoughts to himself. Fujita, too, had made no comment. He seemed to sense his companion's feelings and the two men travelled in silence as the Navy driver hurled the little FWD-drive vehicle along the narrow roads at breakneck speed on dimmed lights.

They were dropped off outside the main gates of the Imperial Dockyard and Fujita insisted on a quick nightcap before returning to their hotel. Taking Bergman into a small bar, he sat him down at a table and ordered a bottle of *sake* for himself and a bourbon for his friend. They drank in silence for several minutes until, thawed by the burning liquor in his belly, Bergman emerged from his mood of depression.

'What are my chances of a trip?' he asked suddenly.

Fujita looked puzzled. 'On what?' he asked.

Bergman glanced round the bar, leaned forward across the table, and lowered his voice. 'On Sendai's little toy - you know, the Tokyo Torpedo.'

Fujita smiled. He appreciated his friend's attempt to keep the name and nature of the *Kaiten* secret although, in his own mind, he was satisfied that no one in Sasebo was likely to turn traitor. Perhaps in Europe one needed to be more careful.

'Fairly remote, I'd say, Konrad,' he shrugged. 'I was surprised you were even allowed to go out on exercises in 202 today. Our security is very strict. But as I know Sendai so well, I'll do my best to talk him into it.'

Bergman swallowed his bourbon quickly. He disliked American liquor but it was not polite to tell Fujita. His pulse was beating faster as an idea began developing in his mind.

'Tell him I did a special course in hydrostatics when I was at Heidelberg University,' he lied. He'd never been to Heidelberg in his life and his knowledge of hydrostatics was limited to the standard course taken by all U-boat officers. 'If I could handle a Tokyo torpedo for myself, I think I will be able to advise him on this flooding problem; I have a theory but I need to make my own observations.'

Get your hands on one. That was the first step in Bergman's plan. Find out how to pilot a *Kaiten* and the rest would be easy. You had to walk before you could run.

'I'll certainly tell him.' Fujita sounded impressed. 'I'm

sure Sendai will welcome some outside expertise. Our scientists seem involved in so many projects at the moment that submarine experiments are very low on the priority list. In any case,' he added spitefully, 'I expect the army pays them more than we do.'

Bergman stood up and stretched. Tomorrow promised to be a busy day and he needed to be fighting fit. And that meant an early night.

'Let's go back to the hotel, Mitsuru,' he said and yawned. 'I need my sleep even if you don't.'

Fujita got his feet reluctantly. There was still some *sake* left in the bottle and he had planned to take his friend to a cabaret show later - the nightclubs of downtown Sasebo were something no self-respecting sailor should miss. He followed Bergman to the door with a doleful sigh of righteous self-denial.

The city was under strict blackout. After Doolittle's raid on Tokyo in 1942, the Japanese civil authorities lived in terror of further attacks on their homeland's sacred soil and no effort was spared to reinforce Japan's defences against the USAF. The fact that the American bomber fleet was primarily a day-attack force did not enter their calculations at any time and as a result of their panic, Japan's home defences were unnecessarily strained by Tokyo's demands for day and night vigilance.

A dusk-to-dawn curfew ensured that no one was permitted on the streets except naval patrols and various odd groups of servicemen returning to their barracks and Bergman found the lonely city strangely unnerving. For some reason, he was reminded of the night when he, Hans Kirchen and Josef Vargas had become involved in a fight with three SA men in Kiel. And it came as something of a shock to realise that his two companions on that memorable night were both dead - victims of the U-boat war. The realization triggered his own survival instincts and he felt the short hairs on the back of his neck rising as they turned into a narrow alley.

His eyes peered anxiously into the blackness as imagined shadows moved in darkened doorways and his footsteps quickened unconsciously. Fujita, however, was irritatingly slow, as if reluctant to get back to the hotel. Stopping in the centre of the narrow passageway, he fumbled in his pocket for a cigarette, pulled out a crumpled packet, and stuck one in his mouth.

The match flared briefly as Mitsuru cupped his hands to shield the flame but the momentary light was sufficient to bring Bergman into action. A black shadow in the doorway to his right suddenly moved and, instinctively, he sidestepped and ducked.

His unexpected evasion threw out his assailant's aim and the lead-weighted cosh struck his left shoulder a paralysing blow that numbed his arm for a few seconds.

'Fujita! Lookout!'

The Commander reacted to the shouted warning with the speed of a cobra about to strike. Stamping one foot forward in front of the other like a fencer about to lunge at an opponent, Mitsuru raised his right hand in a strange palm-down attitude. To Bergman, brought up on the orthodoxies of European fighting, it looked a ridiculous and ineffectual defence. But a moment later, Fujita's hand darted forward and as he ducked beneath his attacker's flailing arms, he struck the man across his unprotected throat with a short chopping movement.

The man dropped to his knees with a choking gurgle and without changing his stance, Fujita jumped into the air to face the second figure. This time, his chopping blow was parried by an assailant who was obviously equally versed in the arts of Oriental fighting but, serenely unperturbed, the Commander half-twisted his body, gripped the man's arm below the elbow with both hands, and threw him against the adjacent brick wall with a force that threatened to break every bone in his body.

Bergman was too busy to follow the rest of the action. Someone was coming at him from the left and, weaving expertly, he threw a straight right. The Kapitanleutnant was a former Baltic Fleet boxing champion and despite his lack of practice, he had forgotten none of his old skills. The granite fist connected with his assailant's chin and the man slithered to the ground with a groan. But there was no time to rest on his laurels.

He sensed rather than saw the flash of the knife and dispensing all thoughts of valour, Bergman threw himself to the pavement and kicked hard at the man's groin. The toe of his shoe sank satisfyingly deep into the soft body and he heard the man shriek as he dropped the weapon. Scrambling to his feet, he kicked again as the Japanese collapsed on the ground and doubled up in agony.

Bergman's humanity had been deadened by years of unrelenting war. Once involved in a struggle for survival, he became little more than an unemotional fighting machine. Ramming his foot into the man's upturned face, he ground the steel-tipped heel of his shoe into the opened mouth. Unmindful of his own horror when, many years before, he had watched a group of SA men brutally beating up a Jewish shopkeeper, he raised his foot and gathered his strength for another savage kick.

Fujita grabbed his arm and pulled him away. 'Let's get the hell out of here while we can,' he urged breathlessly. 'There's at least four of them and we won't stand a chance.'

Bergman glanced around in the darkness. Fujita was right. Two of the ambushers were already stirring and a third was obviously stalking them unseen in the shadows. He sensed, too, that there were others closing in and he knew that next time they'd come in for the kill.

'Right - I'm with you.' He nodded. 'Which way?'

Fujita pushed him towards another alley running off to the right between two towering warehouse blocks. It looked even less inviting than the present passage.

'Down there! Turn right at the end and you'll find the hotel about fifty yards down the road on the left. Come on!'

But despite Bergman's initial forebodings, no one attempted to follow. Their mysterious attackers were disinclined to face up to the two officers again without support from reinforcements although one, a trifle braver than his companions, started off in pursuit.

'Leave them!' Colonel Tagawa ordered curtly. 'And get Akitsu into the car.'

'Do we let them go?' Naganami asked as he helped the Colonel lift the groaning Akitsu into the back seat of the car parked discreetly at the entrance to the alley.

Tagawa nodded. His face was bleeding where Fujita had hurled him against the brick wall and two of his prominent front teeth were broken.

'Yes,' he said thickly. 'Let them go. I can deal with Commander Fujita in my own way and the German officer will not survive for very much longer. I can promise you that Kapitanleutnant Bergman will be dead before his submarine leaves Japan.'

EIGHT

The bruise on Bergman's cheek still throbbed painfully as he hauled himself through the upper hatch and climbed out onto the bridge. I-202 was pounding steadily southwards through the Kondo Channel, the blue exhaust smoke from her diesels polluting the windless air and drifting lazily astern where it hung like a protective canopy over the silvered wash bubbling from her propellers.

The sea was sluggish and the sun reflecting from its mirrored surface gave it the copper sheen of molten metal. Bergman could smell the heat and he swore softly as a steel stanchion burned the palm of his hand. Standing alone on the port side of the conning tower, he watched the shimmering outline of the Kyushu coast slowly vanish into the haze while he assembled his thoughts.

It had been a busy day. And if his plans matured, the afternoon promised to be even more hectic. Turning towards the bows, he stared down at the two *Kaitens* clamped securely to the foredeck. Identical twins and yet vitally different. Hyuga's weapon was fitted with the standard *Type-93* enriched oxygen engine while *No. 2,* the *Kaiten* he had examined in the creek the previous day, was the modified version powered by a hydrogen-peroxide unit. And Bergman had already decided that it was *No. 2* he wanted.

He felt strangely alone without Fujita. But for some unknown reason, the little Commander had failed to put in an appearance for lunch and Sendai, anxious to carry out the afternoon's exercises, had refused to wait for him. Not that it really mattered now, Bergman thought thankfully. Fujita had done his job and, unwittingly cast in the role of traitor, had carried out the first step of the plan with commendable success.

Visiting SUBEXDIV 14 after breakfast that morning, the Commander had bearded Sendai in his office and convinced him that Bergman was one of Germany's leading experts on hydrostatics. And he dropped a broad hint that the Kapitanleutnant was already certain he had found a solution to the flooding problem.

If Bergman was given permission to pilot a *Kaiten,* Fujita had added cunningly, he would guarantee presenting the Captain with a detailed report together with drawings for a new valve relay system within twenty-four hours.

The bait was too tempting to refuse and Sendai had nodded his assent to the proposal without thought for the possible consequences of his action. It was a decision made in haste upon which he was to later repent at leisure.

Bergman shrugged. Knowing Mitsuru's partiality for *sake*, he had little doubt that the Commander was in some waterfront bar drinking himself into a happy stupor. Or - and just as likely with his prodigious sexual appetite - he was amusing himself in one of Sasebo's many day-and-night brothels. Whichever form of escape he had chosen, Bergman felt quite sure that Fujita was enjoying himself.

The incident in the alley the previous evening had, however, reawakened the Kapitanleutnant's old fears that his life was in danger. For some reason, Fujita seemed convinced that the men taking part in the ambush were *Kempei Tai* agents and although Bergman had no proof either way, he suspected the Commander was right. The curfew regulations were strictly enforced throughout Japan and it was unlikely that anyone without the appropriate authority would dare to be on the streets after sundown. And the sound of the car engine starting - an unusually rare noise in wartime Japan - suggested the attack was part of a carefully planned and officially authorized assault.

Bergman made no mention of the ambush to Von Schroeder when he had returned to *U-885* that morning. After all, he reasoned, if the *Kempei Tai* were trying to kill him, there was little doubt that they were acting on the orders of the Gestapo. And that was a personal matter between himself and Gruppenfuhrer Gorst - a matter that would have to be resolved one way or another when he returned to Europe.

But in the privacy of the U-boat's wardroom, he had taken the opportunity to indicate his plans to the Executive Officer so that *U-885* could respond instantly when he finally gave the word.

Von Schroeder made no comment as the skipper outlined his scheme but his eyebrows raised a fraction. Bergman was taking a hell of a chance and if anything went wrong, he didn't like to imagine the consequences. And it was not only Bergman's life which was at stake. *U-*

885 and every man aboard her faced the same risk of disaster. Von Schroeder pushed the doubts from his mind and listened attentively as the Kapitanleutnant told him precisely what to do. You could only die once, he consoled himself.

As I-202 swung east towards the exercise zone, Bergman pushed himself away from the bridge rail and walked slowly across to Captain Sendai. In his own mind, he had already decided to make this a dummy run - a chance to familiarise himself with the *Kaiten*'s controls and characteristics before the main attempt later. No point in taking unnecessary risks, he reminded himself cautiously. And if he could convince Sendai that his nonexistent expertise could solve the problem of maintaining trim, he was confident that every facility would be placed at his disposal when the chosen time came.

'You understand what to do, Kapitanleutnant?' Sendai asked as Bergman joined him. 'You will be embarking in five minutes.'

'I think so. Hyuga has explained the controls to me and I picked up a few tips in the workshops yesterday. If you have experience of submarine handling, there should be no difficulties in driving a *Kaiten*.'

'Don't be too overconfident, my friend,' Sendai admonished with a shake of the head. 'They're unpredictable little bastards. It's like a man having if off with a seventeen-year-old nymphomaniac after twenty years with his wife. They might be built the same way but they tend to react differently. So don't take any unnecessary risks. I don't want to see another one of my *Kaitens* end up on the bottom of the ocean.'

The arrival of I-202's senior radio operator interrupted the homily. He said something to Sendai and handed him a signal slip which the Captain read with increasing bewilderment. He frowned, read it again, and said something to the radio operator who saluted smartly and vanished back down the conning-tower ladder.

Bergman had not understood a word of the conversation and the Japanese symbols scrawled on the yellow signal slip meant as much to him as a coded message without a cypher key. But it was obvious from the expression on Sendai's normally calm features that the signal contained disturbing news.

I-202's captain seemed uncertain what to do. Crumpling the signal into a ball he gripped it tightly in his hand, clasped his arms behind his back, and paced the narrow bridge in silence. Suddenly he stopped, hurled the ball of paper into the sea with an angry gesture, and turned to Bergman.

'Commander Fujita has been arrested,' he explained briefly.

Bergman's mind raced ahead as he hurriedly rearranged his plans in the light of Sendai's unexpected bombshell. 'By whom?'

'By the Imperial Navy Intelligence Section acting on information received from the *Kempei Tai*.'

What the hell good will that do them, Bergman wondered.

'Anything else?' he asked casually. The signal had been considerably longer than this solitary piece of information. And he needed more facts before confirming the decision already forming in his mind.

Sendai hesitated as if reluctant to reveal anything further. Then taking a deep breath, he stared out over the molten copper sea.

'They want to know if you are aboard *I*-202.'

'And...?' prompted Bergman.

'I am to place you under immediate arrest and bring you back to Sasebo for questioning.'

Bergman heaved a sigh of relief that sounded entirely genuine.

'Is that all?' he asked easily. 'What a lot of fuss about nothing - Mitsuru and I were involved in a fight with the *Kempei Tai* last night on our way back to the hotel. Case of mistaken identity.' The Kapitanleutnant contrived to look angelically innocent. 'Well, you'd better do your duty, Captain. Although it's a terrible pity ...'

'What is?' Sendai demanded sharply.

'Well, I'm quite certain I know how to cure the flooding trouble you're having with the *Kaitens*. But if we have to cancel today's trials, I won't have time to sort it out for you. I must sail for Germany on the first tide in the morning.'

The struggle taking place in Sendai's mind was reflected in his eyes. As a patriot, he wanted to do what was best for his country. But as an ambitious career officer he knew promotion would follow if he could tell the authorities how to overcome the *Kaiten's* faults. He had little love for the *Kempei Tai* and he saw no reason why they should be allowed to rob the Emperor of the one weapon that promised victory - and, just as important, to deprive him of this chance of flag-rank. 'What do you suggest?' he asked cautiously.

'I suggest we carry out the trials as planned. I'll wait at the Main Channel buoy and you pick me up and place me under arrest as soon as the experiment is over. I should have time to sketch out the modifications that are needed while we're on our way to Sasebo.'

Sendai considered Bergman's suggestion carefully.

His inborn sense of discipline told him to obey orders. But his common sense nudged him into the Kapitanleutnant's way of thinking. Almost any risk was worthwhile if it promised to turn the *Kaiten* into a viable weapon. And if Admiral Nelson - an admired figure in the Japanese Navy - could turn a blind eye why couldn't a post-captain?

'I give you my solemn word as a German officer that I will be waiting at the Main Channel buoy,' Bergman said quietly as he read Sendai's thoughts. His eyes, clear and blue, looked straight into the Captain's face with candid sincerity.

'Very well.' Sendai nodded. 'But there is no time to waste. You must embark immediately.'

'There is just one other thing,' Bergman said slowly.

'What?'

'May I send a signal to my Executive Officer? I must hand over command to von Schroeder and also inform him of my arrest so that he can report it to our ambassador. Merely a formality, you understand,' he added disarmingly, 'but we have strict regulations in these circumstances.'

Sendai nodded impatiently. 'Very well, Kapitanleutnant - but hurry. There is no time to lose.'

You can say that again, Bergman thought as he hurried down the ladder and made his way to the radio room. It was fortunate that Kakuta, *I-202's* senior wireless operator, knew a smattering of English. It had not occurred to Bergman that the language barrier could have made a total mockery of his plans. But for once his luck held good.

It had only taken a moment to note the vital information he needed and one quick glance at the chart in the control room had been sufficient. He ripped a slip of paper from the pad, scribbled out a signal in German, and handed it to Petty Officer Kakuta with a brief prayer that the man could not read the language.

'Priority,' he said in English. 'Send on 4995 kc's. Understand?'

The wireless operator scanned the paper and nodded. The words meant nothing to him and he assumed they were in code. Reaching towards his transmitter, he twisted the knobs to obtain the required signal band and began tapping out the call sign. Moments later, Bergman heard Gamheim's acknowledgement piping through the receiver. Thank God they were on the alert in U-885.

'Repeat the signal twice,' he told Kakuta. 'Top secret. Understand? Destroy papers afterwards.' He made tearing gesture with his hands and the wireless operator grinned.

'Understand, sir. Send twice. Tear paper. No worry. I carry out orders.'

Bergman patted him on the shoulder and hurried back to the bridge. If anything went wrong now, arrest by the *Kempei Tai* would be the least of his worries.

Sho-i Hyuga was already waiting by the *Kaitens*. He was wearing baggy cotton trousers and had the traditional white scarf wound around his head. He greeted the Kapitanleutnant with an enthusiastic grin. The hatches on top of the *Kaitens* were open and the deck-handling crew was lined up and waiting.

'You take Number One,' Bergman said casually. 'I think I ought to have the unlucky number.'

Hyuga bowed. Bergman's knowledge of Japanese psychology was improving with experience. Hyuga's *No. 1* had survived when Umikaze had been lost the previous afternoon and the young Japanese sub-lieutenant naturally accepted that Bergman, as the guest, was entitled to the honour of taking the new and untested machine. The fact that his *Kaiten* was powered by the *Type-93* motor while *No.* 2 was fitted with the hydrogen-peroxide engine never crossed his mind.

Bergman insinuated his broad shoulders into the narrow opening of the hatch and wriggled his way through the maze of pipes and machinery to the driving seat. The hatch door clanged shut and he shivered as he heard the bolts being secured - an ominous sound that reminded him of screws tightening down a coffin lid. It was an apt analogy. *Kaiten No.* 2 was one of the latest suicide models from which there could be no escape once the top and keel hatches had been externally sealed. Until outside hands released the hatches at the end of the trial, he was a helpless captive inside his steel cigar-shaped prison.

The *Kaiten's* cockpit had been designed for a Japanese pilot and Bergman's large frame was unpleasantly restricted as he settled into the bare metal saddle. The unwinking dials of the instruments stared up at him and the upright bar of the steering column nestled between his legs. Apart from a small battery lamp hanging a few inches above his head, the interior of the Tokyo Torpedo was in complete darkness and Bergman's world was suddenly reduced to three square feet of cold unfriendly metal that smelled of fresh grease and dampness.

Reaching forward, he picked up the headphones of the telephone link and placed them over his ears.

'Report instrument readings, Number 2.'

Bergman read off the dials one by one, checked the fuel level, and carried out the standard pre-launch briefing routine in accordance with the order. He was glad of something to take his mind off the claustrophobic loneliness of his tiny coffin.

'Stand by to submerge,' Sendai warned through the headphones. 'I will launch *Number One* in ten minutes precisely. You will follow exactly one minute later. Good luck.'

The telephone went dead and Bergman switched off the battery lamp to conserve power. *I-202* tilted below the surface and there was a soft swish of water against the *Kaiten* hull as it was carried down riding piggyback on its mother ship. The temperature began dropping as the sea swallowed them into its womb and Bergman shivered again. He must be the world's biggest bloody fool to take such an appalling risk, he told himself. Over the years he had built up a reputation as the U-boat skipper who never took a chance. Yet here he was, locked inside a torpedo with no means of escape, being dragged down to the depths of the ocean at the mercy of a man who had been ordered to arrest him if he survived. He concluded that he was a loser whichever way the coin fell.

It was utterly impossible to see anything inside the *Kaiten* and the relentless drip of water needled into his brain until the monotonous rhythm brought him to screaming point. Groping for the switch, he reached up and turned on the lamp.

The dim yellow beam of light revealed bilge water swilling around his feet and, fighting down his first sensation of panic, Bergman found the pump and set it in motion. The vulgar squelching suck of the diaphragm brought a strangely reassuring comfort and he settled down to wait. Thank God the bloody thing was working. He sighed and glanced at his wristwatch.

Three minutes. He shifted awkwardly on the hard steel saddle and a projecting air pipe jabbed him rudely in the kidneys. He swore as he banged his head on the curved bulkhead plating and he shifted his legs a few inches to ease an attack of pins-and-needles.

How the hell did the *Kaiten* pilots endure this torture for two or three hours at a time? It was worse than sitting in the Nuremberg Iron Maiden. Bergman always liked to be master of any situation he found himself in - it gave him a comforting assurance of survival. But in his present plight, he was no more than a helpless puppet operated by unseen hands completely beyond his reach. Despite the damp chill inside the miniature submarine, Bergman felt himself sweating. And in an effort to take his mind off his fears, he started to run through Hyuga's instructions again and again like an exorcist repeating a catechism to ward off evil spirits.

'Number Two?'

The crackling of Sendai's voice in the headphone concentrated his thoughts.

'*Number Two* reporting. All secure.'

'Check and set rudder.'

Bergman gripped the control stick and carefully centred the rudder. At the crucial moment of launch, the rudders of both the *Kaiten* and mother-submarine had to be in complete alignment.

'In line, sir.'

'Launch in thirty seconds. Your course will be two-eight- zero.'

'Did Hyuga get away okay?'

'Not yet - forward clamps are jammed.'

Rather him than me, thought Bergman. Perhaps *No.* 2

was the lucky one today. It had better be, he decided grimly.

'Stand by ... five ... four ... three ... two ... one ... clamps clear! Start engines. Launch off!'

Bergman pulled the lever that released the final securing catch and pushed the ignition button. There was a momentary delay as the relay valve opened and his pulse raced with tension but, obediently, the torpedo engine whined to life and he felt the machine lurch away from *I-202's* deck.

The *Kaiten* jinked violently to the left and then swerved viciously to starboard with a spine-snapping jerk that nearly threw him out of his seat. It was like riding an unbroken horse and Bergman hung on to the controls with grim determination as he fought to bring the 8-ton monster to heel.

It reminded him of the first time he had driven a car on ice and it did not take long to discover that the *Kaiten* required similar delicate handling. The violent oscillations settled down into a series of untidy skidding swerves and by the time he had brought the weapon under some sort of control, the perspiration was streaming down his face.

The speed was frightening at first and nearly half a minute passed before Bergman remembered the two-position throttle setting. Forward for battle speed, back for cruising. His left hand pulled the lever and the throbbing power of the engine fell away smoothly as the *Kaiten* slowed sedately to 20 knots. Wiping the sweat from his forehead, he let out a heartfelt sigh and settled back in his seat to check the instruments.

Fuel reserves ample ... pressure steady ... roll indicator horizontal... trim stabilised. Glancing down at the

magnetic compass swinging gently in its brass bowl
between his legs, he eased the control lever to port and
corrected the *Kaiten's* course. His watch indicated exactly
one minute elapsed time from launching - that meant he
was almost a mile ahead of *I-202* already. Perhaps he
should indicate his position to reassure Sendai that everything was okay.

Pulling the control stick into his lap, Bergman felt the
Kaiten's bows rise as the diving planes angled the weapon
upwards. Bergman realised he had surfaced too much as
he heard the sharp slap of waves against the hull and he
eased the column forward to dive the weapon gendy into
the depths again.

The sea consumed the torpedo in a swirl of bubbles
and Sendai swore excitedly as he watched Bergman's
ham-fisted driving technique through *I-202's* periscope.
The Kapitanleutnant was maintaining course but it was a
pity he'd not learned to hold the *Kaiten* under control as
well! Bergman's crazy antics reminded him of a playful
porpoise. And he would have felt no great surprise to see
the *Kaiten* leap clean out of the water.

By the time he had travelled two miles, Bergman had
discovered how to maintain an even depth and bracing
the control column between his knees, he took the opportunity to review the situation.

The fact that Sendai was watching him through *I-*
202's periscope was no great worry. Once the *Kaiten*
submerged, the periscope would be useless. But he had to
remember the submarine's hydrophones. *I-202's* mechanical ears would be capable of tracking the torpedo's engine
noises for several miles and Bergman knew that he had to
get beyond sound range before putting the final stage of
his plan into action. Any deviation of course before then

would be detected instantly by the probing hydrophones and Sendai would double back to follow.

But what was the limit of sound range? Two miles . . . three? He decided to allow a wide margin of error and give them five miles. Glancing at his watch, he began mentally to calculate the time. 45 seconds at 50 knots, then eight minutes at 20. That meant he was now at least three miles clear. Another six minutes and he could safely consider changing to his new course. Pity he couldn't throttle up to flank speed but the fuel had to be conserved and there was still forty miles to go.

His mental arithmetic was rudely interrupted as the *Kaiten* lurched to starboard. The roll indicator confirmed a list of thirty-five degrees and Bergman held course while he tried to puzzle out what was wrong. Clearly one of the trimming tanks had begun flooding - probably the midship starboard. Searching down the line of levers on his right, he located the correct control. The vent was in the 'safe' position. Groping alongside his seat, Bergman found the blower controls and he counted along to No. 3. His fingers spread to grip the rim of the valve wheel and he began to turn it gently.

There was a sudden reassuring hiss of compressed air from the pressure lines and he watched the indicators carefully as the needles flickered in response. The white horizontal bar of the roll indicator wavered and began to straighten slowly as the *Kaiten* stabilised its trim. Then, satisfied that the weapon was level again, he screwed down the pressure valve to shut off the compressed air.

Eleven minutes.

Was it time to risk a quick periscope check? Bergman decided against it. Sendai was probably still picking up the faint echoes of the *Kaiten's* power unit and had no reason to suspect that anything was wrong. And if by chance the machine was already beyond hydrophone range, it was silly to give his position away.

Bergman's complacent situation review was sharply shattered by the realisation that the *Kaiten* had lost trim again and was gradually diving deeper into the water. The depth-gauge was already reading twenty feet yet only a few minutes ago they'd been running awash. He pulled the stick back but there was no sign of response. And in those few fleeting seconds, the gauge registered a further fall of five feet.

The controls felt sluggish - like a spoon being stirred in thick porridge - and Bergman knew instinctively that the Tokyo Torpedo was heading towards the bottom. There seemed nothing he could do to counteract the involuntary dive. The *Kaiten* was nose-heavy and the extra weight in the bows was dragging the machine down despite the upward thrust of the planes. Bergman also realised that he had been running for fourteen minutes and regardless of the flooding danger, he had to change course immediately or he would miss his carefully-arranged rendezvous. There were no facilities for navigation in the *Kaiten* and once he deviated from his DR course, he would be utterly lost.

Forcing himself to ignore the needle of the depth-gauge, Bergman pulled the steering rudder to the left, watched the compass swing, and then put the weapon back on its new course as soon as the needle pointed SE by S. In another two hours, he'd know if his gamble had paid off - always providing, of course, that the *Kaiten* had not already started its final death dive to the bottom.

In a desperate effort to counteract the diving angle by using the hydroplanes on the bow section, Bergman hauled the control stick back while he searched his memory to recall what Sendai had told him about the stripped-down *Kaiten* they had examined in the workshops. Little by little the details came back to his mind - the pumps and their positions, the trimming tanks and their capacities, the warhead and its weight.

Bergman sat up with a jerk. The warhead - that was it! That was the cause of the trouble. The Japs were obviously making the same stupid mistake as the Royal Navy had done in 1914. Their trimming calculations were based on the lightweight practice head and they had completely overlooked the fact that the combat warhead weighed more than twice as much. And bearing in mind that a fully-equipped *Kaiten* carried 1,000 pounds of explosives in its nose section, the difference was considerable.

But discovering the cause of the problem did not stop the weapon from sinking and Bergman's survival now depended on remaining calm and finding his own salvation.

Leaning back in the seat, he began recreating the plan of the *Kaiten* in his mind while he calculated the precise effect of the heavier warhead on the weapon's trim. Then, holding on firmly to the mental picture, he worked out the trimming adjustments necessary to compensate for the greater weight in the bows. It was an intricate calculation and in *U-885* it was normally worked out by the Executive Officer with the aid of a slide rule. Bergman's face perspired with the mental effort required but his brain remained ice-calm as it added, subtracted and multiplied like an electronic computer. And as he checked and rechecked his sums, the *Kaiten* was already nosing down to eighty feet. He felt no panic and calmly reminded himself that the frail steel hull would start yielding to the crushing pressure of the sea at any moment if he failed to act soon.

Reaching down, he twisted the valve wheels and began blowing the port and starboard tanks simultaneously. He recalled Hyuga's warning: 'Once you blow the tanks, the air reservoirs are exhausted. If you dive again, you will never surface.'

Bergman mentally shrugged. He only needed to blow them sufficiently to restore trim. And he now knew the precise amount required. The air hissed through the lines and although he had no instrument to tell him, he knew instinctively that the bows were levelling off. It was almost like riding a horse by the seat of one's pants but as an experienced submariner, he could sense the attitude of the submerged vessel simply by feel. Perhaps that was where the *Kaiten* pilots had failed - not one of them could match his experience.

Twisting the valves shut to conserve his precious supply of high pressure air, Bergman tried the hydroplanes again. The engine behind his back continued its steady whine and by the faint beams of the battery lamp, he saw the needle of the depth-gauge rising slowly but surely. The *Kaiten* was already at thirty feet and she was lifting at the rate of ten feet per minute - ridiculously slow by submarine standards but a bloody sight better than the previous inexorable descent to the ocean bottom.

Bergman's head was throbbing as the limited oxygen supply dwindled and the stale air, heavily contaminated with carbon- monoxide, made breathing difficult and painful. Yet despite the physical discomforts, he experienced a feeling of elation. Now that trim had been restored, the *Kaiten* answered every touch of the helm and Bergman knew he had conquered it. There was a bitter irony in the situation. He had solved the weapon's flooding problems in obedience to his promise to Sendai but the Japanese would never know.

Killing the solitary light, he returned the hydroplanes to the midship's position. The Tokyo Torpedo responded sweetly, levelled out, and held a steady running depth just beneath the surface.

So far as Bergman could estimate, he had a margin of eight hours in which to make his escape. It would take Sendai four hours to return to the creek and there was bound to be further time lost while they decided whether the *Kaiten* had accidentally sunk or whether the Kapitan-leutnant had hijacked the weapon. And knowing the Japanese propensity for red tape, he gambled on a further two hours respite before any attempt was made to mount a search. By that time, his possible location could be anywhere inside an arc of 4,000 square miles.

Reaching up, he pulled the periscope into position and pressed his face against the eyepiece. Visibility had fallen off considerably since the launch and a mist was gradually building up over the sea. An excellent cover for escaping his hunters but a further complication to the already difficult task of locating the waiting *U-885*. Bergman wiped his sleeve over the eyepiece and cursed the poor quality of Japanese optical glass - it was like looking through the bottom of a milk bottle by comparison with the precision Zeiss optics used in German periscopes.

Running awash at a steady 20 knots, the *Kaiten* continued to hold its SE by S course while Bergman kept a wary watch for patrolling surface ships and aircraft. The mist was still closing in and by the time the hands of his watch indicated an elapsed time of three hours, visibility was down to three miles. But supremely confident of his navigation, Bergman killed the engine as he reached the featureless emptiness of the rendezvous point.

The *Kaiten* rolled sluggishly in the swell but she was not drifting. Bergman sighed with relief. A surface wind or a tidal current of as little as two knots could have made nonsense of his carefully-calculated course and diverted him anything up to twenty miles from his DR position. And now, with the modicum of luck which the Kapitan-leutnant regarded as almost a matter of divine right, *U-885* should be circling within visibility range at any moment.

Bergman had known it to be a wild gamble all along and even now he could not be entirely sure of final success. Anything might have happened to upset his hastily-laid plans. The executive order he had signalled to von Schroeder could have been deliberately sabotaged by *I-202's* radio operator. Or, suspecting trickery, the Port Admiral at Sasebo might have prevented the U-boat from sailing. And of course there was always the possibility of a last minute mechanical failure.

His headache was getting worse and the stale oxygen-starved air inside the *Kaiten* made the effort of breathing progressively more difficult. Bergman had experience of being trapped in a sunken submarine and he knew the warning signs. Inside another fifteen minutes, he would lapse into unconsciousness and the great plan would have failed.

Von Schroeder had posted extra lookouts at the bow and stem of *U-885* in addition to the normal duty men on the bridge. The U-boat was cruising slowly on the surface at five knots but the swirling banks of mist made the task of locating the hijacked *Kaiten* virtually impossible and the Executive Officer knew that he dared not prolong the search beyond the thirty-minute time limit set by the Kapitanleutnant. Everything depended on the probing beam of the radar search receiver and he glanced up at the silent sentinel of the *Hohentwiel* scanner on its pole above the bridge. He had little faith in German radar equipment but at least it gave him one more pair of eyes. It was lucky that Taussig had purloined sufficient bits and pieces from the electrical depot at Sasebo to make the bloody thing work again.

'Radar contact, sir!'

Kosch passed the message up through the hatch gnd the Executive Officer lifted the bridge telephone.

'What do you have, Taussig?'

'There's a very small blip on the surface about a mile to starboard - object appears to be stationary.'

'Hold it and track!' Still gripping the telephone in his right hand, von Schroeder bent over the voicepipe.

'Steer eight points to starboard. Engines dead slow ahead.' He looked up. 'Taussig's made radar contact,' he shouted to the lookouts. 'Keep your eyes peeled!'

U-885 nosed her bows through a thick patch of mist, broke into pale watery sunlight for a few moments, and then glided back into the swirling fog again.

'Contact lost, sir!' Taussig reported on the bridge telephone. 'Too much surface scatter - the screen looks like a bleeding snowstorm.'

Damn the bloody radar! It always played the fool just when you needed it most, thought von Schroeder. What chance did they have of finding the *Kaiten* in this fog?

'The skipper's not far away now, lads,' he encouraged the lookouts. 'Keep searching.'

U-885 slid quietly out of the fog bank into another area of clear daylight and the watching men screwed their eyes in protection against the sudden glare of the sun.

'Object dead ahead - four hundred metres!'

Von Schroeder's hands trembled as he lifted the binoculars to check Zimberg's sighting report. He focused on a small object bobbing gently up and down on the grey sea. It was low in the water but there was no doubt about its torpedo shape. And the thin stalk of periscope standing up from the humped midship's section was the final confirmation. By Christ! They'd done the impossible. They'd found the skipper!

'Stop engines. Holst - steer one point to port.' *U-885* lost way as the diesels died and she drifted towards the *Kaiten*. Bottcher and Hartmann took up position in the bows and stood waiting with boat hooks ready to grapple the tiny submarine alongside. Willi peered down at the floating cylinder but could detect no sign of life.

'Kosch! Secure the boom of the derrick and stand by. You know what to do.'

The U-boat's derrick was housed under the deck plating close to the main hatch forward of the conning tower. Its sole purpose in life was to load torpedoes into the forehatch. But now it was about to be used in a way its designers had never dreamed of.

Willi Hartmann jumped neatly on to the *Kaiten's* bows as Bottcher hooked it skilfully against *U-885*'s ballast tanks. The boom swung out and he quickly secured the lifting chains to a ring bolt in the nose. Then, moving aft, he attached the other hook to the stem ring. He raised his arm to indicate that the task had been completed.

Von Schroeder swallowed hard. So far everything had

gone like clockwork. But this was the moment of truth. The *Kaiten* weighed all of eight tons and the derrick boom was designed for a maximum lifting capacity of three. Could it stand the strain? The Executive Officer felt a little like an angler holding a very small net under a hooked fish and hoping he'd catch it.

Petty Officer Kosch shared von Schroeder's misgivings. He licked his lips nervously as he waited the signal to start lifting. It would be a cruel stroke of fate to lose the skipper at the very last moment.

'Haul away!'

The electric motor of the crane whined to life and the boom creaked as the securing chains pulled taut. No one spoke but all eyes fastened on the steel links to see if they would hold. Kosch moved the lever gently and the boom groaned under the strain as it began to lift. Hanging in the water, the *Kaiten* seemed reluctant to leave its natural element but inch by painful inch, it rose upwards to expose its black underbelly.

'Gently, man, *gently*!'

The Oberbootsmann thrust the lever forward as the *Kaiten* swung awkwardly clear of the water. He could smell the motor overheating and hear the grumbling creak of the chains straining under the excessive weight. Easing the controls back, he watched the steel cylinder rise another two feet. Then slowly, very slowly, he swung his precious load inwards towards *U-885's* deck.

'There's the keel hatch,' von Schroeder said and pointed. 'Get it open quickly - the skipper's probably choking to death in there.'

Brecht reached up and tightened his wrench over the head of the first bolt. It moved easily and released the safety stop of the hatch-securing bar. He grasped it with one hand and swung it clear. Then releasing the two butterfly clips, he pulled the hatch-door open.

A cloud of poisonous yellow fumes funnelled out of the circular hole and he turned away gasping as he took the full blast. How the hell could anyone still be alive in that muck, he asked himself as he bent over and coughed his lungs up.

Taking a deep breath, Hartmann thrust his upper body into the hatch and emerged a moment later dragging Bergman's legs out through the opening. He sagged under the weight and Kosch ran to help. Between them, they manhandled the skipper's limp body out of the *Kaiten* and laid him carefully on the U-boat deck. His face was sheet-white and his eyes were closed but as Hoyt bent over to check his pulse he detected a faint flicker of life in Bergman's stubborn body.

Taking a small vial from his emergency kit, the Sanitasobermaat snapped the glass neck and handed it to Zimberg.

'Hold it under his nose, Manfred, while I get him breathing.'

Straddling himself across the Kapitanleutnant's hips, Hoyt placed his hands on each side of Bergman's ribs and began slowly pumping. He could not be sure if it would work but he had to try and there was a long silence as the men watched and waited.

Bergman's body suddenly jerked and he twisted his head to escape the acrid fumes from the vial which Zimberg was holding under his nose. Then, with a tremendous effort, he heaved himself upright into a half-sitting position. His eyes opened and he began coughing; without warning, he was violently sick over the deck.

Apart from the gentle lapping of the sea against the

U-boat's iron sides and the sound of Bergman retching, the U-boat's deck was completely silent. The men gathered quietly into groups and stared at the apparition of the man who had returned from the dead. No words seemed adequate to express their relief. And it was left to Willi Hartmann to reduce the scene to anticlimactic banality.

'We'll know if the old bastard's still alive when he tells us to clear that mess off the deck,' he said cheerfully and Bottcher nodded.

Bergman wiped his mouth with his sleeve and grinned weakly to Hoyt as the Sanitasobermaat took his arm and helped him up.

'Good to see you back, sir,' von Schroeder said quietly. 'I'm glad that's all over. And I daresay you are as well, sir.'

Bergman took a deep lungful of fresh salt air. The colour was returning to his face and his eyes were bright.

'Don't get too optimistic yet, Number One. We're not out of the woods by any means. There's another 12,000 miles to go before we can say it's all over. And we'll be fighting every inch of the way!'

The Kapitanleutnant was definitely feeling better. The pounding pain in his head had eased and it no longer hurt to breathe. Pushing Hoyt's guiding arm away, he stood rock solid on his own two feet and looked round.

'Hartmann!' he barked.

'Sir?'

'Clean that bloody mess off the deck!

NINE

U-885's fore-end's had lost its customary exuberance. Bottcher was already snoring defiantly on his bunk while the rest of his companions sat quietly around the scrubbed wooden mess table drinking mugs of cocoa.

'Watch it for Christ's sake!'

Hartmann snatched his hand away as the Sanita-sobermaat dabbed a pad of iodine on the raw palms.

'Sit still, Willi!' Hoyt gripped Hartmann's forearm tightly as he cleaned up the torn flesh. 'You might have the Iron Cross but you make more fuss than a bloody baby.'

He placed a strip of lint on the hand and sealed it down with an adhesive plaster.

'You'll live,' he said unsympathetically.

'That's what you think,' Willi grumbled. 'You want to try lifting eight tons of submarine and see how you feel.'

'I've ruptured me bloody self,' Brecht broke in determined not to be outdone by his messmate in the agony stakes. 'Me - with a brand new wife waiting for it as soon as I get back to Kiel. Just my bloody luck.'

Hoyt looked up with interest at the opportunity to try his skills on a new patient.

'Would you like me to check?'

'How?' Brecht asked suspiciously.

'Get your pants off and I'll examine you.'

'Look out, Hugo,' Hartmann warned with a grin. 'The bastard just wants an excuse to tickle your balls!'

'That's right, Hugo. Cough for the nice doctor!'

Brecht grabbed himself defensively and, forgetting his affliction, he backed away from the Sanitasobermaat like a bull retreating before a toreador.

'Keep your bloody hands to yourself,' he warned Hoyt. 'I'll manage it somehow. I'll make Gerda do all the work herself.'

'That's the way he likes it,' Willi grinned at the others. 'You should have seen him lying back and enjoying it when we were in Penang. That's the trouble with you, Hugo. You're even too bloody lazy to shag properly.'

Manhaussen climbed through the bulkhead hatch. Like the others, his face was black with grease and the sweat had cut white streaks into the dirt. His left hand was bandaged and there was a plaster on his cheek.

'Break it up, lads! The Captain wants you fit and fresh in the morning so let's get some sleep.'

No one argued. They were too exhausted to grumble. And the Obergefreiter's order was a perfect excuse to climb into their bunks without losing face. Even Hartmann obeyed. Putting one foot on Bottcher's berth, he hauled himself up to the top position alongside the polished steel body of a reserve torpedo. His back felt as if it was breaking but, as usual, he was determined to have the last word.

'If the skipper wants his bloody Tokyo Torpedo moved again tomorrow, you can tell him to get stuffed.'

But nobody laughed. The rest of the fore-end's mess were already fast asleep from the exhaustion of their labours.

Von Schroeder's eyes were also drooping wearily. As the Executive Officer, the U-boat's trim was his responsibility. And with eight tons of extra weight lashed to the upper deck, *U-885* was dangerously unstable. It had taken several sheets of closely-calculated figures to compute the necessary changes in the position of the water ballast but, spurred by the knowledge that the U-boat was unable to submerge until the calculations were completed, he forced his tired brain to function. How the devil Bergman had found the mental stamina to work out the *Kaiten*'s trim in his head was something he would never understand.

In the absence of a third deck officer Kosch, *U-885*'s coxswain, had been assigned to Watchkeeping duties and while von Schroeder supervised the alterations in trim, Kosch and the lookouts stood Watch on the bridge.

The faint hiss of water and the gentle throb of the pumps moving the ballast from one trimming tank to another had a soporific effect on von Schroeder but he forced himself to stay awake until the task was completed. He had never imagined it possible to feel so exhausted. The strain of guiding *U-885* out of the Sasebo dockyard had started the rot. And the fear of failing to locate the *Kaiten*, heightened by the unexpected fog, had completed the process of utter mental exhaustion.

Yet despite his personal weakness and fatigue, Bergman had insisted on having the *Kaiten* lifted on board the U-boat and then securely lashed for the long passage that lay ahead. On top of everything else, it had seemed an impossible task. But Bergman had given the lead and everyone had buckled down. Three weeks ago the crew would have mutinied in the face of the demands that he'd made upon them. Yet not a man had grumbled when the skipper gave his orders and everyone, even Hartmann, had put their backs into the job.

It had taken over two hours to nestle the eight-ton monster onto the wooden chocks which Badenholdt had carefully prepared in one of the dockyard sheds the previous morning. The derrick had given up the ghost halfway through and the final lifting had been done by the aching muscles of the men strung out down the length of the deck like a tug-of-war team - heaving, swearing and sweating as they struggled with the steel hawsers.

Torn hands and livid bruises were the only rewards for their efforts to manhandle the *Kaiten* on board but Bergman allowed no respite. The job had to be completed by sunset. And it was.

Von Schroeder sighed at the memory but he felt a certain pride in their achievement. Without Bergman's driving determination, they would have never made it. But they had - and that was all that mattered. He walked wearily to the bridge voicepipe and whistled up Kosch.

'I'm turning in for a few hours,' he told the coxswain. 'The trim should be all right now but I can't work bloody miracles so if anything seems wrong, call me immediately. I want you to remain on the surface all night and make sure the batteries are fully-charged. We'll have the entire Japanese Navy chasing us tomorrow and we'll probably be submerged and running on the motors all day.'

Von Schroeder ducked through the circular hatch in the aft watertight bulkhead, stopped for a quick word with the radio operator, and then pushed through the curtains into the wardroom. Kicking his heavy sea-boots into a corner, he pulled off his shirt and started to climb into the sweat-soured bunk. What had the skipper said earlier? Twelve thousand miles to go. The Executive Officer's mouth twisted in a sardonic grin. He couldn't see the Japs letting them go 120 miles once they guessed that Bergman had hijacked a *Kaiten*. And yet - and this was the ironic twist to the whole situation - unless they actually *saw* the U-boat with its stolen prize, they could never be quite sure.

FIVE HOURS of uninterrupted sleep was a welcome luxury for a combat U-boat officer and von Schroeder felt completely refreshed as he climbed back onto the bridge at eight bells. It still needed an hour or so till dawn but it gave him time to check the various routines before they dived.

'There's some Jap destroyers scouting around about ten miles to the southwest,' Kosch reported. 'Taussig's been tracking them on his radar since midnight.'

'Any indication they know where we are?'

'Not so far as I can tell. They seem to be running an east-west patrol - about seven miles on each leg. As soon as I confirmed the pattern, I changed course to run parallel.'

'Good man,' von Schroeder said. He glanced up at the ugly flat mesh scanner of their radar receiver. No wonder the Allies were winning the war, he thought to himself. If that obsolete *Hohentwiel* equipment could keep them from tangling with the Jap destroyer patrol, just imagine what those new microwave sets could achieve. He turned to Kosch. 'Anything else?'

'Gamheim reported a lot of signal traffic to the north but it's been quiet for the last couple of hours. Too quiet, if you ask me.'

'Radio silence, you mean?'

'I reckon so.' Kosch nodded. 'And that means the Japs know we're somewhere around.' He yawned and stretched. 'Well, I'll leave you to it, Oberleutnant. The batteries are fully-charged and the old girl's ready for whatever the skipper wants. I'm off to my bunk. I was dreaming about Garbo last night and I want to enjoy the interesting bits before we get sunk.'

Cheerful sod, von Schroeder grumbled to himself as Kosch slid down the ladder to the control room. He felt a pang of envy at the calm way the more experienced members of the crew faced the dangers of their present situation. Personally, he was plain bloody scared. After what the Japs had done to the American prisoners at Balabac, he didn't relish the thought of being captured. But he didn't want to die either.

Bergman's arrival on the bridge fifteen minutes before sunrise took his mind off the terrors that still lay ahead. Once the Kapitanleutnant was around, there was little time left for morbid thinking. He made his report and drew attention to the destroyers Taussig had located on *U-885's* radar. Bergman nodded but made no comment. He stared down at the ugly grey slug lashed to the foredeck. Then he straightened up.

'All hands to clear the bridge. Stand by diving stations.'

Von Schroeder hurried below followed by the lookouts. Bergman heard the diesel engines fade away and then the hum of the electric motors. A sudden roar of water told him that the main vents had opened and almost simultaneously he felt the U-boat settle slowly into the sea. Taking a final survey of the surface horizon where the pink fingers of dawn were clawing upwards in the east, he climbed into the hatch, pulled the cover down, and secured the clips.

'Thirty feet - half ahead both. Steer one-eight-zero.'

Thyssen trimmed the U-boat level at thirty feet and as the repeater telegraph tinkled in the motor room, Venne eased the rheostat switch to half power.

Von Schroeder bit his lip nervously as the helmsman swung the wheel and brought *U-885* onto her new course. No captain likes his orders questioned. And by reputation Bergman was unduly sensitive in this respect. But he knew he had to do it.

'The new course will take us directly towards the destroyer patrol line, sir,' he pointed out.

'I am quite aware of the fact, Number One. We should have broken through the line last night while it was dark - now we'll have to do it submerged.'

'But I thought Kosch did the right thing in holding a parallel course to their track.'

'Perhaps that's why you've not been given a command appointment,' Bergman bit back unkindly. 'The Japanese have no radar on their destroyers and if we had used our scanner to pinpoint their position in the darkness, we could have cut through them at high speed on the surface and got clean away. Now we've got to sneak past them in daylight and that means creeping underneath submerged. I need not remind you that while they have no radar, they have very efficient hydrophones.'

'But why due south, sir?' von Schroeder persisted.

'Why not hold our previous course down through the China Sea?' Bergman walked across to the chart and nodded for the Executive Officer to follow. His finger traced the reciprocal line of their outward course down the west coasts of the Philippines and Borneo.

'We would be walking into a trap. Once committed to the South China Sea route, we have only two means of exit - the Malacca Straits or the Sunda Strait between Java and Sumatra. The Japs could seal off either passage without difficulty.' His finger traced another line south and then westwards. 'But this way - keeping the Philippines to starboard - we've got a hundred and one possible routes into the Indian Ocean. And I've got to break south now so that we can pick up our refuelling junk north of Luzon. If we don't make our rendezvous, U-885's bunkers will run dry somewhere around the Cape. And I have no intention of making the British Navy a present of our Tokyo Torpedo.'

'He's dead ahead, sir.'

Bergman turned away from the chart table as Konstam reported the propeller noises.

'Take her down to two hundred feet, Number One. Maintain course and speed. Secure for depth-charge attack.'

U-885 nosed deeper and von Schroeder watched the gauges as the big red needles fingered down. At least there was a certain satisfaction from the fact that the U-boat was holding her trim - his calculations were on the ball even if his courage was lacking.

'Good trim, Number One,' Bergman acknowledged appreciatively.

The U-boat levelled at 200 feet and glided silently towards the line of destroyers crisscrossing the surface.

'Slow ahead both.'

The soft whine of the motors died to a whisper. There were two muffled thuds in the distance but *U-885* was well beyond danger range.

'Those two were at least three miles away,' Bergman said reassuringly. 'The Japs are probably dropping random patterns.'

A thundering roar belied his words. The U-boat rocked violently under the concussion and there was a tinkle of broken glass. Bergman stood at the telephone checking off damage reports. He seemed unconcerned and made no effort to alter course or speed. The interior of the cramped control room was as quiet as a grave as the men waited for the next explosion.

'Random,' he said succinctly. But he knew no one believed him.

'HE directly overhead.'

'Motors dead slow - cut pumps. Rig for silent running.'

The whispering hum of the motors faded into nothing and only the almost imperceptible tingle of the vibrating deck plates indicated that *U-885* was still under power. The groaning squelch of the pumps, croaking in unison like a chorus of marsh frogs, stopped abruptly as Baden-holdt shut down the master switch and the U-boat pushed lazily through the depths at a bare two knots.

The undertow of the Japan Current sweeping north-easterly from the Philippines swung *U-885*'s bows to the left and Bergman saw Holst moving the helm to counteract it.

'Let her go, Steuermann,' he instructed quietly. 'Follow the direction of the drift - we'll get more speed that way.'

'Four knots, sir,' von Schroeder confirmed from the Patent Log.

Another violent concussion struck the hull like a giant sledge hammer. U-885 rolled to starboard as if she'd been kicked by a mule. More light bulbs shattered but the main power remained on. There was an ominous sound of water leaking through sprung plates in the forward compartments.

'Pumps, sir?' Badenholdt queried.

Bergman shook his head. 'Negative! Any sound and they'll pick us up immediately. They obviously don't know we're smack bang underneath them and they're just dropping their charges at routine pre-set intervals.'

Although the U-boatmen trusted their skipper's skill, there was not one of them who did not consider Bergman's assessment of the situation over-sanguine in the circumstances. The waiting was the worst part of it - not knowing whether the enemy had them pinpointed and if the next explosion would rip open the fragile hull and send U-885 plunging to the bottom for the last time.

The humidity inside the submarine sent the hygrometer off its scale and trembling droplets of moisture had built up on every surface. The pallid grey faces glistened wet with sweat and the strain showed in the hollowed questing eyes and nervously twitching fingers. But Bergman's assessment had been right. The threatening thuds of the exploding depth charges faded further and further into the distance as U-885 was swept eastwards by the fierce current until, finally, even Konstam's sensitive mechanical ears lost contact.

'Full ahead both. Steer one-eight-five.'

'Group up! Full ahead!'

'One-eight-five, sir.'

'Pumps, sir?'

Badenholdt's question broke Bergman's concentration. He'd forgotten about the leaks. He nodded.

'Yes, Chief. Start the pumps. And get me a damage report from the bow compartments.'

An hour later, Bergman decided to risk another radar probe. The U-boat came up to periscope depth and, sitting on his saddle in the armoured command tower directly above the control room, he made a quick sweep of the horizon while Taussig was ordered to search north and west.

'No contacts, sir.'

'Are you sure that bloody set isn't on the blink again?'

'Yes, sir. Functioning normally.'

Bergman leaned back from the eyepiece of the 'scope and spoke into the voice pipe.

'Stand by to surface. Duty Watch to close up.'

'Close main vents - planes hard a'rise!'

'Blow all tanks!'

U-885 broke surface in a sullen calm on a sea of dark molten lead. Not a breath of wind stirred the air and there was an oppressively heavy feel to the atmosphere. Bergman glanced around the horizon, uncomfortably aware of impending trouble. He could not define it but he knew it was there.

'Remember, lads - anything you see means potential danger. The Japs are after our blood and they control the entire area from here to the Indian Ocean. And don't forget the enemy either. If you spot a ship or an aircraft, it *must* be hostile. Understand?'

The lookouts nodded and resumed their stations with a new awareness. Bergman watched them and smiled to himself. What a difference in attitude from that abominable passage out to Penang.

It was Bottcher, standing starboard bow lookout during the Afternoon Watch two days later, who demonstrated the new keenness by making a sighting.

'Captain to the bridge.'

Bergman raced up the ladder and joined von Schroeder on a starboard side. The Executive Officer pointed to a smoking object in the middle distance and Bergman's blood ran cold as he raised his binoculars. He stared out over the sea for a full half-minute and then lowered them.

'If the Japs can't sink us, they obviously intend to starve us out,' he observed enigmatically.

But how the hell did they know? His thoughts went back to the last time they had refuelled at sea after leaving Balabac. There was no possibility of a security leak from the crew - apart from the officers no one had been allowed ashore at either Tokyo or Sasebo. The muscles of Bergman's jaws tightened. Fujita was the only other person who knew they were using disguised trading junks to top up their bunkers. And it was obvious that the Japanese had deliberately sought out and attacked Heinekker's boat in an attempt to leave the U-boat low on fuel.

And only Fujita could have given them the information they needed. It was too late for regrets but Bergman wondered whether his friend had warned the Japanese authorities of his own free will or whether the *Kempei Tai* had tortured the information out of him.

The burning junk drifted downwind and, lifting his glasses again, he could see the bodies heaped grotesquely on the flimsy poop and the great steering oar swinging freely. The holes punched into the reed mat sails and the splintered woodwork of the hull testified to a surprise air attack against which the junk could offer no defence. And ripped by cannon fire, the telltale length of red silk fluttered lifelessly from its stem quarter.

'Continue on course, Number One. And maintain maximum speed.'

Bergman had no intention of telling anyone the real significance of the wrecked junk. It would be disastrous for morale if they knew *U-885* now faced the prospect of running out of fuel by the time they reached the Cape. And whatever else might happen, he had to keep the U-boat at fighting pitch. During his long years of combat command, the Kapitanleutnant had developed a fatalism that, a few months earlier, would have been completely out of character. But as he had learned by bitter experience, opportunities had to be grasped without time for thought where and whenever they presented themselves. And setbacks had to be accepted with a similarly unthinking shrug. If they were destined to get back to Germany with their prize, something would happen. And if not, it was up to him to find a suitable place to scuttle his boat so that his men had a fighting chance of survival.

Leaving von Schroeder on Watch, he slid down the ladder into the steamy heat of the control room.

'How much longer is that damned port motor going to take?' he demanded irritably as Badenholdt emerged through the hatch from the motor room naked to the waist and dripping with sweat.

'The armature's burned out, sir,' he explained casually. 'The motor was running hot after the depth-charge attack - the jolt of the explosion probably threw it out of line. My boys are working on it. I'd give it a couple more hours at least.'

Badenholdt was a good engineer. A former senior technician of a world-famous electrical combine in the Ruhr before the war, there was little he did not know about electric motors. But he wasn't a submarine man and the urgency of the situation had made little impression.

'A few hours is too long, Chief.' Bergman tried to hide his irritation but it left a sharp edge to his voice. 'We're coasting the eastern side of the Philippines at the moment and we're well inside the range of Japanese shore-based aircraft - not to mention a score of destroyers. We can just about dive with one motor but that's all. And until we can operate at maximum capacity underwater, this bloody boat's a sitting target for anything the Japs care to throw at us. I know your boys have a difficult task on their hands but that motor must be running within two hours.'

Badenholdt sighed wearily. Bergman could be an inhuman slave driver when it suited him but he accepted that the skipper had good reasons for his demand. Wiping his hands on a piece of cotton waste, he nodded and ducked back through the hatch.

Bergman glanced down as Kosch pushed a clipboard in front of him.

'Have you seen the met readings, sir?'

He frowned at the figures and looked up sharply. 'Are you sure these are correct, Cox'n?'

'Yes, sir. I showed them to Murcken and he advised me to pass them to you immediately.'

Erich Murcken was *U-885's* second bosun. A reservist called back to the Navy in 1939, he was a professional seaman by trade and had served with Hamburg-Shanghai Steamship Company before the war.

Despite his Petty Officer rating, Bergman had made use of his expert local knowledge on more than one occasion.

'I've seen these sort of readings before, sir,' he confirmed quietly. He looked serious. 'I think you know what they mean.'

'A fairly bad storm,' Bergman opined casually. 'Although I must admit, I've never seen the pressure drop so fast even in the North Atlantic.'

'It's more than a storm, sir.' The control room went suddenly quiet as the men listened. Murcken was an old 'China hand'. He knew what he was talking about as a rule.

'Well?'

'It's a typhoon, sir.'

Bergman had never been in the Far East before but in his days as a cadet, he could recall seeing the old Jean Harlow and Clark Gable film *China Sea* at a cinema in Kiel. And the memory of the typhoon - even though it was manmade in a Hollywood studio - had remained vividly in his mind ever since. He nodded his thanks to Murcken, handed the clipboard back to Kosch, and hurried up to the bridge.

The horizon to the south and southeast was choked by swelling black clouds spreading like angry bruises across the blueness of the sky. The molten metal sea was stirring in a sullen swell and a rising wind whipped white spray from the tips of the waves.

'Looks like we're in for a good blow,' von Schroeder greeted him with a nod towards the storm gathering ahead.

'I'll take over the Watch,' Bergman said curtly. 'I want four of our toughest men on lookout - and get some more lashings around the *Kaiten*.' The Executive Officer saluted and swung himself into the hatch. 'And send Badenholdt topsides,' Bergman added as a passing shot.

U-885's bows began to plunge more steeply as the sea rose and there was a frightening majesty about the inexorable march of the black sky. Visibility was already dropping and as sharply violent squalls passed over the U-boat, the wind mounted in its intensity.

Badenholdt's face came up through the hatch and he looked anxiously at the skipper. What the hell was wrong now? He scrambled onto the bridge with a sigh. If the Old Man wanted the motors fixed, he'd have to curb his impatience and stop dragging him away from the task every few minutes. Bergman said nothing. But grabbing the engineer's shoulders, he twisted him towards the bows and pointed.

'You're looking at a typhoon, Chief. And the only way we can survive is by submerging. Now get that bloody motor of yours working - and quick!'

The sight of the swirling storm ahead brought a new urgency to the situation. Badenholdt knew all about typhoons - he was an avid reader of Josef Konrad. And he knew that a cockleshell craft like a submarine with its low freeboard and minimal buoyancy stood no chance against the powerful forces of nature.

'We could finish winding the armature when we've submerged, sir. I can get the starboard motor connected up and running in fifteen minutes.'

'Do it!'

Bergman wasted no words. There was no time for anything but immediate and relevant action. An unpleasant chill had crept into the heavy atmosphere and the bracing wires were beginning to tauten and whistle in the rising fury of the wind. White foam was now flying from the wave crests and the entire horizon was a black backcloth of swiftly moving clouds that towered upwards like giant mountains tinged with blazing gold as they slid across the sun.

'Strap yourselves in position!' Bergman bellowed as the new lookouts tumbled up the ladder to the bridge. Von Schroeder had picked his men well: Bottcher, Hooschlant, Thyssen, and Steine - the toughest and most experienced crewmen on board. Flapping across the deck in their black oilskins, they took up their stations and clipped the patent safety harness around their waists. Another oilskin was passed up through the hatch and Bergman climbed into it.

'Secure the hatch, Number One!' He had to shout to make himself heard above the rising scream of the wind. 'Call me as soon as we can dive. And keep a deck party ready in the control room in case I need them.'

U-885 dug her bows into a wall of water and the sea surged down the foredeck to vent its fury against the unyielding steel ramparts of the conning tower. Surging back with an angry roar, it renewed the onslaught and hurled a wall of water over the bridge. Bergman clung to the rails as the U-boat rolled under his feet and he shook his head to clear the salt spray from his eyes. How long did Badenholdt say - fifteen minutes? He doubted whether they could last half that time.

He had few fears for the U-boat itself. Germany built her submarines to stand up to anything. But there was always the danger of the typhoon lifting the heavy steel hatches so that she flooded - or swinging her bows so that she broached beam onto the maelstrom and capsized. If she did, the Duty Watch on the bridge stood little chance of survival and the men battened below under sealed hatches even less.

U-885 leaned stiffly under the increasing power of the wind and dipped her bows deeply into the boiling sea. It was impossible to see more than a hundred yards in any direction from the low vantage point of the U-boat's bridge and the mast-high waves were building solid walls of black water around the pitching submarine that seemed to defy penetration. Nothing was visible but the lashing terror of the storm.

Bergman felt his way to the front of the bridge. The spray tore his face like a million frozen needles and with every plunge of the bows, the force of the water crashing down over the conning tower brought the Kapitanleutnant to his knees, doubled over and gasping for breath. It was difficult to see where the sea ended and the deck began and a tumbling angry tumult of water hissed, boiled, and foamed beneath the conning tower. But as the sea fell away before renewing its strength for a fresh assault, he could see the *Kaiten* still securely lashed to the deck and riding the back of its steel steed like an armoured valkyrie racing wildly to Valhalla through the teeth of a Teutonic storm. And there was, indeed, a Wagnerian magnificence in the gargantuan strength of nature's unleashed power.

U-885 twisted violently as the wind changed direction. A savage gust tore the bows sideways leaving the weather-side brutally exposed to the full force of the typhoon's primeval energy. Cold stinging water cascaded over the submarine in a never-ending torrent, knocking Bergman's feet from under him and sending him sprawling and gasping against the high steel side of the bridge. Bending his head like a charging bull, he fought himself upright and clawed blindly for the voice pipe. The noise was indescribable yet through the shrieking wind and the pounding roar of the sea, he heard a faint scream. The wind snatched the fleeting sound away almost before it had registered in his brain and Bergman had no time to consider what it presaged. Clinging tightly to the voice pipe, he ripped out the plug and thrust his mouth against the open tube.

'Full power, Number One! I must have speed!' He shook his head and spat water from his mouth as *U-885* took another enormous wave over her starboard beam. 'Steer two points to starboard - we're broaching! Get the bows round, man.'

Von Schroeder added his own urgency to the command as he repeated it to the men in the control room.

'We're full ahead already, sir,' he reported back. 'The propellers are coming out of the sea each time the bows go down - the Chief says we'll strip the clutch if you don't ease off.'

'To hell with the clutch! Keep her on maximum revolutions!' Bergman clung desperately to the voice pipe as another freak wave washed over the bridge. His body felt bruised and battered as if he'd just lost a fifteen-round boxing contest with Max Schmeling. His hands were bleeding and his eyes stung with salt. 'Get those damned bows round!'

'I've got three men at the helm, sir, and even then we can't hold it. Steuermann Holst broke his arm when the wheel went wild - it's sheer bloody bedlam down here.'

'It isn't much fun on deck either,' Bergman said sourly with studied understatement.

The pounding crash of the sea on the beam eased as

U-885's bows moved sluggishly into the wind but it brought little relief for the group of men fighting for their lives on the exposed bridge. The deck was knee-deep in black water and as each wave ebbed noisily through the scupper drain holes, the undertow threatened to drag Bergman's legs from under him. He wondered how the lookouts were faring and he suddenly remembered the warning shout and despairing scream. Hanging grimly to the bridge rails, he looked back towards the stem.

Bottcher's station was empty and only the torn webbing of the safety harness remained to show the cause of the tragedy. Bergman checked that the other lookouts were still at their stations and then turned away.

The eighteen-stone giant must have been ripped from his straps by the same wave that had thrust the bows sideways a few minutes earlier. And he had no possible chance of survival even if there was time to stop and turn back. The white spumy surface of the wind-torn sea rose and fell with sickening ferocity as if digesting its hapless victim while the shrieking wind howled a shrill lament for the lost man. *U-885* heeled violently to port as another mountainous sea crashed down with a terrifying roar and in the general tumult Bergman heard a sharp crack like a gun being fired. He peered forward into the black driving rain.

One of the steel hawsers lashing the *Kaiten* to the foredeck had parted under the strain and the stem of the Tokyo Torpedo shifted ominously as *U-885* bucked and twisted under the battering fury of the typhoon. Another wave like the last would hurl it overboard into the raging seas to be lost forever.

Bergman had no intention of being robbed of his prize and he was willing to accept any risk to save it. He could not stand by and see it vanish over the side like the unfortunate Bottcher. Men were expendable - the *Kaiten* was not.

The steady roar of the diesels suddenly faltered. They misfired, spat defiantly, and then faded away. Bergman grabbed for the voice pipe and tore off the cover.

'What the hell's happening, Number One?'

'Exhaust uptake carried away, sir.' Von Schroeder sounded breathless as he made his report. 'We're taking water into the engine room.'

'Close the high induction valve,' Bergman instructed. The U-boat was in immediate danger of flooding if the exhaust trunk was not sealed off quickly. Clinging to the bridge rails, he waited for von Schroeder's confirmation.

U-885's bows swung wildly at the mercy of the mountainous seas as she lost power and he could hear the hawsers securing the *Kaiten* creaking under the strain. The tortured sounds forced him to decide.

'Flood all tanks and submerge,' he told von Schroeder. 'I know it's risky but we can't remain surfaced without power. Start the routine and open up the hatch.'

U-885 was at the mercy of the sea gods. Battered and helpless, buffeted by the wind and pounded by the mountainous waves, she wallowed in the surging spray-wracked water like a mortally wounded whale waiting to die. Bergman could do nothing more to save her. It was now just a matter of fickle chance whether the U-boat could flood her tanks and submerge beneath the surface before the typhoon rolled her over and sent her to the bottom in a lurching dive from which there could be no hope of recovery.

'Clear the bridge!'

Hooschlant and Steine unsnapped their harnesses

and clambered back across the slippery deck as the U-boat rolled and plunged in the boiling seas. A fifty-foot wave crested down on the hapless submarine, hung motionless for a brief second, and then crashed with the weight of a falling wall as Thyssen unfastened the buckles of his safety straps to join them at the hatch.

The men hunched themselves into balls and clung to the deck rings as the sea roared down. It was like standing beneath Niagara. Their heads pounded, their eyes stung with salt, and they gasped for breath. And as the foaming water gurgled and drained into the scuppers Thyssen had vanished.

Bergman pulled the locking lever clear and dragged the heavy counterweighted hatch cover back. He recoiled as a blast of hot stinking air struck him in the face and the sour smell of vomit made him retch. Fighting back the nausea, he pushed Hooschlant down into the narrow opening.

'Hurry - get below!'

The seaman dropped through the hatch and Steine followed close behind. Bergman slid his legs into the opening, found the rungs of the ladder with his feet, and reached up for the hatch cover. Looking upwards, he saw another enormous wave about to break and he slammed the lid shut as the sea swirled hungrily across the empty bridge.

'All tanks flooding, sir,' von Schroeder reported as the Kapitanleutnant descended into the control room. He looked as white as a sheet as U-885 rolled wildly. 'We've no steering or directional control.'

Bergman's sea boots slithered as he walked across to the telephone. Looking down, he saw the floor of the control room was covered two inches deep in an evil sludge of bilge water, diesel oil, and reeking vomit. Although it hadn't struck him so at the time, the Executive Officer's earlier report of conditions inside the U-boat had been just as understated as his own.

'Thirty feet, sir.'

'Keep flooding.'

Even at a depth of thirty feet, the turbulent water reflected the awesome power of the typhoon on the surface but at least the worst of the violence was cushioned. *U-885* continued to roll and pitch but the momentum of the movements was dampened.

Bergman had the control room telephone in his hand when he felt the deck plates vibrate softly beneath his feet.

'Sir?'

Badenholdt's head stuck through the opening in the watertight bulkhead. His face was gleaming with sweat and he was naked to the waist. His chest was caked with dried vomit. But he was grinning.

'Yes, Chief?'

'Motors connected and running, sir.'

'What the hell took you so long?' Bergman grinned back.

He cradled the phone back on its hook and glanced at the depth gauges. Then wading through the stinking mess on the floor, he checked the gyro repeater.

'Stop flooding at fifty feet. Steer two-zero-zero. Half ahead both.'

'Close vents - stop flooding!'

'Steering two-zero-zero, sir.'

'Group up - half ahead both. Reserves sufficient for twelve hours running at half speed, sir.'

Back in her true domain beneath the sea, *U-885*

resumed her stately if slow progress while the typhoon ripped and tore the surface of the Pacific Ocean in a final paroxysm of frustrated anger. For the first time in three hours, Bergman sat down in his special canvas chair just behind the helmsman to enjoy the luxury of relaxation. His hands were bleeding, his face bruised, and his eyes swollen and bloodshot from the fury of the sea. Lifting his feet clear of the revolting mess swirling aimlessly across the deck, the corners of his mouth lifted in a rare smile.

Having won his battle with the elements, Bergman was suddenly quite content with his lot.

TEN

'Reply from *BdU*, sir.'

Bergman took the decoded signal from Gamheim and digested its contents at a glance. It was brief and to the point. And it was no more than he had expected.

FROM BDU TO CO U-885. 09-14.12 May 43
IMMEDIATE

Your 08-46 of today refers. Seehund Group withdrawn from areas M-164 to M-198. No supplies available. Good luck.

Kom. Schiller for BdU.

HE FOLDED the slip of pink paper neatly, thrust it into his hip pocket, and slowly paced the narrow width of the bridge.

U-885 had beaten the odds this far but Bergman had

known all along that his luck could not last forever. He had outwitted the *Kempei Tai,* stolen a *Kaiten,* survived the typhoon, and then successfully run the gauntlet of Japanese sea and air patrols through the Molucca and Flores Seas before finally ducking through the unprotected Lombok Strait into the vast wastes of the Indian Ocean.

Even the stopover at the Cocos and Keeling Islands where the U-boat had spent three days licking its wounds while the crew repaired the worst of the storm damage had been uneventful.

But now his luck had run out. And that bastard Schiller was having the last laugh.

U-885 had taken eighteen days to cross the enormous span of the Indian Ocean - eighteen days during which they had sighted nothing either living or dead - and Bergman carefully maintained a steady twelve knots to economize on their precious fuel. But realising that the moment of truth could not be delayed indefinitely, he had finally passed an urgent signal to U-boat HQ in Paris requesting an immediate rendezvous with one of the supply U-boats operating off the east coast of Africa. He had deferred his request to the last possible moment but with only three day's oil left in her bunkers, *U-885* was on her last gasp and like an explorer lost in the desert with an empty water bottle, disaster was inevitable unless fresh supplies could be obtained. And now *BdU* had told him the cupboard was bare.

'What next, sir?'

Although von Schroeder had not seen the contents of the signal, it was not difficult to guess the message it contained. And Bergman's face was confirmation enough of its bad news. The Kapitanleutnant stopped pacing up and down like a caged lion and shrugged.

'If the mountain won't come to Mohammed ... I don't need to finish the proverb do I, Number One?' Walking across to the voice pipe, he flipped back its brass cover. 'Steuermann - steer new course three-zero-zero.'

Von Schroeder waited as the course change was repeated and *U-885*'s bows swung towards the northwest. He rubbed his chin thoughtfully. Bergman was running them quite deliberately towards the coast. And that meant an increased danger of encountering the air and surface patrols protecting the Allies' vital tanker route from the Gulf to Britain via the Cape. He began to understand what the skipper meant about Mohammed and the mountain. But with a crippled boat, he was taking an appalling risk.

Their battle with the typhoon had left its scars and the U-boat looked battered and weary as it ploughed northwestwards. The rails lining the bridge were bent and twisted where roaring seas had smashed and pounded them. The small high-powered attack periscope was snapped clean at its base leaving only the large steering 'scope. In itself it was perfectly efficient but its thick bulk spumed unwelcome spray when in use, making the U-boat an easy prey for escorting destroyers. The radar scanner, too, had been swept overboard and *U-885* could no longer rely on the probing eye of the *Hohentwiel* beam to locate its enemies. The same wave had also torn the *FuMB* aerial from its mounting, leaving them with no means of anti-radar defence either.

In fact, the U-boat was virtually blind and although the hydrophones saved it from being deaf as well, their safety now depended on the skill of the lookouts and the cunning of their captain. Rusty and salt-streaked, with a permanent three degree list to starboard that added to the forlornness of her appearance, *U-885* reflected the strains and stresses of her momentous voyage in every inch of her exhausted hull. But she could still fight. And the Kapitan-leutnant had no intention of giving up the ghost yet.

'Ever led a boarding party, Number One?' Bergman asked von Schroeder casually as he resumed the Watch from Kosch.

'Not since my class at the Academy tried raiding the Admiral's wine store on the *Gneisenau* in 1939,' grinned the Executive Officer. 'And I doubt if tomatoes and rotten eggs are suitable weapons these days.'

'Well, you'd better brush up your techniques,' Bergman warned. 'Get a boarding party together and draw automatic weapons from the master-at-arms. And tell Hartmann to check that the *fleschboot* is still seawor-thy. I intend to visit a tanker and have a drink.'

Von Schroeder accepted his instructions with calm resignation. He had long since ceased to be surprised by Bergman's apparently wildcat schemes and like the rest of *U-885's* crew, he had complete confidence in the skip-per's uncanny ability to succeed no matter what the odds. Even so, he experienced a momentary qualm as he reflected on the U-boat's semi-crippled condition.

But even Bergman's exuberant optimism showed signs of waning when the next forty-eight hours passed without even the sniff of a tanker. Twice, SAAF air patrols sent them diving deep to the raucous squawk of the klaxon and on the morning of the second day, he was forced to remain submerged at periscope depth, fuming impotently, as a well-laden Australian convoy chugged slowly down into Simonstown. But attack was out of the question. It was essential for *U-885*'s presence in South African waters to remain as secret as possible and even though Bergman could have snapped up two or three well-laden freighters with a quick salvo of torpedoes, he was in the galling position of needing to spare his enemy if he wanted to survive.

By noon on the third day, the men standing lookout on the bridge reflected the general air of pessimism and they drooped despondently over the rails as the fruitless search continued.

'Only enough left in the bunkers for another twelve hours at cruising speed, sir,' Badenholdt reported gloomily as Bergman took over the Afternoon Watch at eight bells.

'How about the motors?'

'We ran a full charge on the batteries last night, sir. I'd give them around 24 hours at 2 knots. Of course,' he added slyly, 'I suppose I could always get my lads to run up some sails.'

Bergman ignored the Chief's heavy-handed attempt at humour and stared out over the bare horizon. According to their noon sun reading, *U-885* was about fifty miles from the coast and that meant changing course towards the shore by midnight if the crew were to have a chance of survival when he scuttled the U-boat. His mind went back to the wild chase across the Atlantic the previous year when he had deliberately chosen to sail *UB-44* beyond the point of no return in order to claim a victim.

His mouth turned down at the memory. That was in the old days when the death wish sat heavy on his shoulders. But it was different now - that part of his life was behind him. This time he wanted to stay alive even if it meant seeing the war out in a British prison camp. The contingency plan gradually unfolded in his mind - steer NNW at midnight and make landfall in the area of Cape St Lucia. Then, if the batteries held out, crawl slowly up the coast and try to reach Portuguese-controlled Mozambique. Internment was more inviting than being taken prisoner.

'Ship approaching - starboard ninety! Ten miles!'

Bergman snatched up his glasses and pinpointed the stranger. It was a tanker - fat and fully-laden. And it was steaming alone and unescorted.

'Stand by to dive! Clear the bridge!'

Choosing an interception course, Bergman steered towards the unsuspecting tanker and when the range was down to a mile, he poked up *U-885*'s bulky steering periscope to identify it.

The red and green flag painted on the tanker's hull at bow and stem allowed for no errors of identification. And the name, emblazoned on the side in large gold letters, was confirmation of her nationality - *Ponta Delgada*.

'Portuguese!'

'Do we let her go, sir?' von Schroeder knew the skipper's firm views on the sanctity of International Law and respect for neutrality. Bergman had never attacked a neutral vessel in his entire career except those sailing in British convoys which he regarded as fair game and within the rules. But this was different.

Bergman ignored the question and continued to stare through the periscope as he decided his next step. A hungry man did not consider the moral aspects of a situation when he had a chance to steal food. And *U-885* was hungry.

'Stand by to surface!'

'Blow all tanks - planes hard a'rise!'

'Steer two points to port - slow speed.'

'Two points to port, sir. Steering three-five-zero.'

'Group down - slow ahead both, sir. Engines standing by.'

'Gun crews and boarding party to the control room!'

While von Schroeder and the Coxswain assembled their groups, Bergman took advantage of the brief hiatus to finalise his plan of attack. Complete surprise was the first essential and if that was not possible, then at least some sort of ruse to throw his victim off balance. Either way, he had to gain time and stop the tanker from using its radio. And repugnant though the idea was, the Kapitan-leutnant could see no viable alternative to his original idea. It was the oldest trick in warfare - and the dirtiest.

Crossing to the signal locker, he opened the third drawer down, pulled out a flag, and quickly stuffed it inside his shirt. No one saw him do it and certainly no one would have guessed what was in his mind even if they had.

'Lauerbach!'

U-885's yeoman signaller stepped forward and clicked his heels.

'Sir?'

'Hoist the ball and drum as soon as we surface. Then I want you to flash a repeated *KF* at the tanker until they acknowledge.'

Lauerbach nodded, took his signalling lamp from its hook on the bulkhead and joined Bergman on the ladder. Kosch's party was next in line with von Schroeder's boarding crew bringing up the rear. Having checked that the men were in their correct places, *U-885*'s skipper outlined the bones of his plan.

'Kosch - keep the gun crew out of sight behind the bridge screens. If the tanker ignores my signals or makes a hostile movement, I'll give you a shout. If I do, knock the hell out of her! But upperworks only. I don't want her sunk. Gamheim - you stay by your radio. As soon as they send a distress call, I want it jammed. Now does everybody know what to do?'

The men nodded. After weeks of boring routine, they welcomed the chance of some action. And they had got to the point where they would have followed Bergman to hell and back if he ordered them to go.

'Right - this is it!'

The hatch cover thrust back at the precise moment *U-885's* conning tower poked above the surface and, ignoring the surge of cold black water flooding down through the circular opening, Bergman scrambled onto the bridge closely followed by Lauerbach.

The signaller strung his two black symbols to the halyards of the wireless mast and hoisted them. Then, holding the 6-inch signalling lamp to his eye and aiming it carefully at the tanker's bridge, he leaned on the edge of the conning-tower coaming while his finger began beating a staccato tattoo on the trigger:

KF...KF...KF...KF...KF...

Bergman watched the *Delgada* slow and blow off steam. A group of officers gathered on her bridge were staring at the surfacing U-boat and obviously discussing its probable intentions with growing excitement. An acknowledgement flashed back from the tanker's lower bridge and he waited tensely for Gamheim to report picking up the routine U-boat sighting report.

But nothing happened. He frowned as he waited.

Several of the tanker's crew were running to and fro

along the central catwalk in obvious panic while on the tall super-structure of the poop, others maintaining some sort of discipline were swinging out the port lifeboat in readiness for launching. It all looked too perfect, too well-rehearsed, and too good to be true. Bergman suddenly shivered. His mind went back to the way his father had died in 1918. Could the apparently harmless tanker be one of the Royal Navy's deadly Q-ships?

The seeming panic of the crew was typical of the carefully-staged routine which the British had developed to lull the unsuspecting U-boat captain into false complacency. That was how *UC-115* had gone down - pounded into a smoking wreck by the Q-ship's concealed guns which had been unmasked the instant the submarine was in range. And his father had died with the rest of the U-boat's crew in an unmarked grave on the ocean bottom, the victim of the enemy's traditional cunning.

Bergman's binoculars swept carefully along the length of the tanker searching for hidden guns. Everything looked normal enough - no incongruous deckhouse behind which quick-firers could be concealed, no high bulwarks designed to hide 6-inch guns, and no side hatches shielding invisible torpedo tubes. He felt the sweat beading his upper lip as he repeated the survey again.

The Portuguese flag was no guarantee that the vessel was neutral. The British often used the age-old ruse of neutral flags to cover their true identity. International Law only required a warship to reveal its true colours when it opened fire. And by that time is was too late!

As his binoculars swept across the bridge, an insignificant detail caught his eye. He paused, returned his search to the same point, and studied the object with more than usual care. He had found the clue he needed and with sudden decision, he ripped the silk flag from under his shirt and threw it to von Schroeder.

'Run it up - quick. Before it's too late!'

U-885's Executive Officer stared down at the piece of bunting in horrified disbelief. Surely the skipper wasn't serious? To give in tamely without even trying to fight?

'Jump to it, Number One!' Bergman barked, 'Trice it up!'

Lauerbach stepped forward, snatched the white flag from von Schroeder's nerveless hands, and quickly bent it to the signal halyard. Catching hold of the line, he hoisted it so that it caught the breeze and fluttered its shame.

Kosch pushed Hartmann back down behind the bridge screen as he tried to scramble to his feet in protest.

'And you can keep quiet, Willi,' he warned sharply. 'The skipper knows what he's about.'

'So do I. Christ Almighty, that bloody old tub's not even armed!'

Bergman was aware of the growing rumble of discontent behind his back as the news spread amongst the crew but he ignored it and watched the bridge of the Portuguese ship warily. By his reasoning, the white flag should make them stop and think. If the *Delgada* was a Q-ship, the British would be anxious not to miss the chance of capturing a U-boat in full working order and they'd almost certainly hold their fire. On the other hand, if the tanker was a genuine neutral, the white flag would remove their fears of attack and natural curiosity would do the rest.

'They're lowering a boat, sir,' von Schroeder reported.

Bergman nodded and glanced down at Kosch's men crouched out of sight behind the bridge screen.

'It could be a trick,' he cautioned. 'Every British trap-ship carries a specially trained "panic" crew. Their job is to create the impression of wild confusion. And they take to the boats to make us think the vessel has been completely abandoned. So if I give the word, I want to see every record broken in getting the deck-gun into action - there'll be no time for a handling error or misfire. It's a dangerous game and whoever shoots first will probably win the battle.'

'Then why the hell don't we start shooting now?' Willi grumbled to his companion. 'Hit the bastards before they hit us.'

'I'll tell you why, Hartmann.' Bergman's eyes never left the small boat rowing steadily away from the motion-less tanker as he answered the whispered question. 'Because we need oil if we're going to get back home. And if it's *not* a Q-ship, I have no intention of blowing our only source of supply out of the water just because half of my crew has a dose of the shits!'

'They're still heading this way, sir,' von Schroeder said quietly.

Bergman nodded. 'So I observe - but they're fouling their range while they hold that course. And it's exactly the sort of thing they'd do if they were genuine.'

'But if it's a trap-ship?'

'Then they're either bloody brave or incredibly stupid. They'll have to steer to port and get out of range before the guns are unmasked. Knowing the Royal Navy, however, they're quite likely to come close in and chance their luck just to deceive us up to the last possible moment. Don't forget that Q-ship gunners are picked men who hit with their first shot. If they time it correctly, they can keep us on a piece of string until the final seconds.'

Von Schroeder chewed his lip. There were times when he wished the skipper was less of a pessimist. He glanced back at Kosch and noted the sheen of perspiration on his face with smug satisfaction. At least he wasn't the only one with the wind up, he thought thankfully.

'One hundred yards now, sir,' he reported.

It was an unnecessary warning. Bergman was watching the approaching boat with narrowed eyes. He was like a tiger tensing its muscles before leaping onto its prey.

'Kosch! Take Hartmann with you and go down towards the gun. Strip off your shirts and start waving - you know the old shipwrecked mariner's act. But stay near the gun and if I give the word, or if the enemy opens fire, get it into action. The rest of the crew will join you as soon as the other ship shows its hand.'

The coxswain dragged off his sweat-stained shirt, crossed to the after ladder of the conning tower, and started down it. Willi Hartmann followed. He was already naked to the waist but, following the spirit of Bergman's instructions, he waved his skinny arms enthusiastically.

The officer sitting in the stern of the boat stood up and waved back. He said something to the men at the oars and their backs bent with extra effort as the distance closed rapidly.

'More men on deck!' Bergman ordered. 'Try to look as if you want to be rescued.' But despite his apparent confidence, von Schroeder noticed that the skipper kept his binoculars firmly focused on the tanker's bridge as if trying to read the mind of its captain.

The boat nudged against the ballast tanks of the submarine and rolled gently in the swell as if its crew were uncertain what to do next. Kosch made up their minds for them. Acting instinctively and without orders, he scrambled down the weed-covered plating of the tanks and grabbed hold of the bows while Hartmann helped the officer on to *U-885*'s deck. Most of the submarine's crew had crowded onto the stem and in obedience to Bergman's strange instructions, they were leaping up and down, shouting and cheering their erstwhile rescuers.

'So far, so good,' Bergman grunted to von Schroeder as the tanker officer was guided excitedly up the ladder to the bridge by a somewhat over-enthusiastic group of German sailors. 'Looks like she was genuine after all, thank God. Now comes the tricky bit - you know what to do if things go wrong.'

It needed little acting ability on the part of *U-885*'s crew to play the role of survivors. Their clothes were ripped and dirty from the demands of their long voyage and their faces looked gaunt and haggard. Even the U-boat itself reflected the pretence. Listing forlornly to starboard with most of its upper-works mangled and twisted by the force of the typhoon, with red streaks of rust peeling the sombre grey war paint from the plating, the white salt crusting her conning tower and net cutters, *U-885* gave the impression of being on its last legs. And the white flag fluttering fitfully from a makeshift signal mast lashed to the broken stump of the attack periscope mounting only added the final confirmation.

Manuel Gomez, Second Officer of the *Ponta Delgada,* certainly had few doubts in his mind as he climbed the bridge ladder to meet the U-boat's captain. The poor bastards looked all in. He saluted gravely as Bergman stepped forward to greet him.

'You are in distress?' he enquired in halting English. 'You require assistance?'

Bergman nodded. He had not shaved for three days and the worry of the fuel situation had cut deep furrows into his already gaunt features. He looked, in fact, exactly how Gomez had expected him to look.

'Thank God you've found us,' he said brokenly and, taking the Portuguese officer's hand, he squeezed it firmly. 'We've been drifting out of control for at least ten days. Where the hell are we?'

'About forty miles from Mozambique.'

Bergman affected surprise. Wiping his hands wearily across his face, he slumped his shoulders.

'My God ... we were lucky the British Navy didn't get us,' he told Gomez with sincerity that wasn't entirely feigned. 'That's why we hoisted the white flag,' he added hurriedly as if he didn't expect the officer to believe him. 'All our gear's wrecked - we thought you were a British vessel.'

Gomez grinned broadly and clapped a reassuring hand on the Kapitanleutnant's shoulders.

'No danger, *capitano*,' he beamed. 'Portugal neutral. We help you.'

Bergman backed away suddenly. His eyes narrowed suspiciously.

'I must see your captain, *Teniente*.'

'But of course - I will take you to meet him. But why?'

'Special cargo.' Bergman spoke very softly and mumbled the words as if reluctant to give away an important secret. 'I can only tell your captain.'

'Of course, *capitano*. Come, I will take you.'

Bergman started down the ladder towards the waiting lifeboat and then stopped suddenly. He gave the impression of a man shaking himself back to reality after a disturbing dream. Bracing his shoulders, he drew himself erect.

'May I bring an escort?' he asked with disarming politeness. 'I know we are finished - *kaput* - but the traditions of the German Navy require me to observe the proper courtesies even to the last.'

Gomez looked doubtful. He did not suspect the Kapitanleutnant of a trick but the unexpected request threw him off balance.

'There is no room in the boat,' he objected.

Bergman contrived to look angelically innocent. He had rehearsed the words carefully in his mind beforehand and they flowed without effort.

'I am a man of honour, *Teniente.* I am sure you understand how I feel. It is my duty to pay my respects to your captain in the traditional manner.' He shrugged desolately at the wreck of the U-boat. 'It is the least I can do in the circumstances.'

Gomez paused irresolutely and was lost. Unable to resist the request, he nodded his agreement. It did not occur to him at all unusual that the four men who appeared in response to Bergman's orders were fully kitted out in regulation uniforms complete with submachine guns and sidearms. And as they jumped down into the waiting boat, the Kapitanleutnant took a gun-belt from Kosch and buckled it securely around his waist.

Hartmann pushed the nose of the boat away from *U-885*'s fantail, the Portuguese crew paddled her gently astern and then, bending over their oars, they began pulling back to the tanker.

Captain Castilho was waiting at the top of the accommodation ladder as Bergman and his escort climbed up to the deck. He seemed disconcerted by their smart appearance and his eyes narrowed as he saw the guns. But with the typical courtesy of his race, he ignored the implied threat and greeted the U-boat commander with a warm smile. His breath smelled of whisky and Bergman could not resist a complacent smile as he recalled seeing the open bottle and the glasses on the tanker's bridge. It was only a tiny detail but it had been sufficient to convince him that the *Delgada* was not a Q-ship. The Royal Navy might break every rule in the book to disguise their decoy vessels. But they would never permit alcohol on the bridge.

'*Teniente* Gomez tells me you wish to speak privately.'

Bergman nodded. Posting Gunther and Plotz to guard the companionway to the bridge, he, Badenholdt, and the other guard followed the tanker captain up the steps and into the diminutive chartroom. Castilho found another bottle of Scotch, uncorked it, and offered it to the Kapitanleutnant. Bergman shook his head.

'I would like to join you in a toast, Captain,' he explained, 'but these are dangerous waters for a U-boat. I must keep a clear head. May we get to business?'

'Of course. You wish to surrender?'

Do I *fick*, thought Bergman.

'We are not surrendering,' he said aloud. 'And I must apologise for the trick. But I had to ensure you were not a British warship in disguise.'

Castilho nodded and tut-tutted with his tongue. 'I understand, Kapitanleutnant. British very bad using

Portuguese flag. My government, it has made many protests but they take no notice.'

'What's your cargo and where are you bound?' Bergman asked. The tanker captain's wheedling efforts to curry favour irritated him. He was not impressed by neutral protestations. He knew the British used neutral flags to cover their identities. But so did the German Navy when it suited them. And there were no such things as ethics in his book when one was fighting for survival.

'One thousands tons of crude for Lisbon and five hundred tons of refined diesel for Benguella in Angola.'

'What's your price?'

Castilho shrugged. 'I do not know, Kapitanleutnant. The agents arrange prices - I only deliver.'

'All right, I'll believe you. Well, what's the insurance cover?'

Castilho told him after a hurried search through the mass of untidy papers bundled with the cargo manifest in a side locker. Bergman nodded, jotted the figure down on a piece of paper, and made some rapid calculations.

'That's around twenty pounds a ton for the diesel,' he said finally. 'I'll offer you one hundred pounds a ton for immediate delivery.'

The captain's eyes gleamed greedily. 'It is a lot of money,' he pointed out suspiciously. 'But it is a matter for the owners – I cannot make arrangements for the owners.' He spread his hands. 'You understand?'

'No, I don't,' Bergman told him shortly. 'Do we get it or do we not?'

Castilho looked around the chartroom for a means of escape but Obergefreiter Hentschel was blocking the only exit and the barrel of his Schmeisser machine gun looked ominously lethal.

'But I have no authority,' he protested.

Bergman pulled the Mauser pistol from his waist holster and held it casually in his right hand.

'This is your authority, Captain,' he said quietly. 'And I will arrange a one-thousand pound bonus for you in Lisbon if you agree.'

The Portuguese swallowed hard. It was difficult to know whether to be frightened or elated.

'Two thousand,' he countered.

'Very well, Captain. Two thousand pounds bonus and one hundred pounds per ton. I will write out a draft authorising our Ambassador in Lisbon to pay the money on demand. You have only to present it - the Reich Government gives me full power to draw on foreign funds.'

'In American dollars...'

'You can have it in bloody gold ducats if you want to,' Bergman snapped impatiently. 'Now do you agree?'

Captain Castilho held out his hand and smiled.

'But of course, Kapitanleutnant. Who is arguing?'

'YOU COULD HAVE HIJACKED the entire load if you'd wanted to,' von Schroeder observed when Bergman had finished explaining the deal. 'They were terrified out of their wits.'

Two long flexible pipes snaking from the tanker's outlets and slung clear of the surface by means of jury-rigged lines from *U-885*'s battered torpedo hoist snuggled securely into the bunker inlet valves as the black lifeblood pumped from the *Delgada* to the submarine. The U-boat could take 442 tons of oil in her long-range tanks and

Bergman was determined to fill them to the last pint. It was going to cost the German Government nearly £50,000 in precious American dollars but, in his view, it was cheap at the price. What were a few million marks when balanced against the secrets of the *Kaiten*?

He focused his thoughts back to von Schroeder's question. 'Whatever enemy propaganda may say about me, Number One, I am not a pirate. But I had good reasons for what I did. That draft ensures Castilho will do nothing likely to endanger our safety - he won't want us sunk until he's got those dollars firmly in his sweaty little hands. And we'll be home in Kiel long before he reaches Lisbon.'

'Do you mean our Ambassador will actually pay up, sir? I thought you were bluffing.'

'Not at all, Number One. As captain of *U-885*, I have complete authority to incur any expenses necessary to maintain the safety of my boat.' He laughed suddenly. 'I could have paid him £1,000 a ton but you know what we Bavarians are like - we prefer to strike a good bargain.'

The last few gallons of fuel gurgled into the U-boat's brimming bunkers and Badenholdt began tightening the starboard inlet cock while Aachan deftly released the nozzle of the oil line. Throwing a leading rope across to the *Delgada*, they waited for the tanker crew to haul it clear.

Bergman wondered whether they really deserved the prodigious luck they were enjoying. The refuelling operation had taken just under two hours and *U-885* had been surfaced most of the afternoon a mere fifty miles from an enemy-controlled coast. Yet not a single patrolling aircraft or prowling surface vessel had disturbed them at their labours.

Somehow, almost instinctively, he knew they were going to make it safely back to Lorient without further incident. The climax of the mission had been reached and passed - from now on it would be all plain sailing. He could not explain the presentiment but he could feel it in his bones. And he felt suddenly completely confident of their ultimate success.

As he watched Badenholdt secure the final valve and bolt the deck plating back into position, Bergman began speculating on his probable reception when he returned to Europe. He had, for example, deliberately disobeyed Schiller's secret directive although, in the circumstances, there was little the Kommodore could do about that. And Doenitz would certainly disapprove of his piratical action in hijacking the secrets of an honoured ally - in fact, he reminded himself, there was probably a hell of a diplomatic row in progress between Tokyo and Berlin at this very moment.

But the *Kaiten* would compensate for all his sins. And when the *Grossadmiral* recovered from his initial annoyance, he had few doubts that Doenitz would recognize the value of his hard-won prize. Looking ahead, he could even foresee the day when the Kriegsmarine would establish its own midget submarine flotillas.

And he wondered what the expression on Gruppenfuhrer Gorst's face would be when he learned that his old archenemy had survived again. Bergman grinned to himself. He was almost looking forward to his next clash with the evil Gestapo chief who had hounded him so mercilessly for the past two years.

'Captain Castilho, sir.'

Bergman looked down to see the Portuguese officer standing expectantly on the deck. He resembled a swarthy South American taxi driver waiting for his tip in the red light district of Rio. The Kapitanleutnant acknowledged his arrival with a curt nod and leaned over the voice pipe to call up Klauer, U-885's wardroom steward.

'You'll find a box of Dutch cigars in Number Two locker, Hans. Bring them to the bridge, please.' He paused and then grinned with sudden inspiration. Lowering his voice, he gave Klauer some further instructions.

Castilho beamed his thanks as Bergman came down the ladder bearing his gifts. He took the cigars with a bow and his eyes glinted greedily as the Kapitanleutnant handed him a carefully-wrapped brown paper parcel.

'The cigars are with the compliments of the Kriegsmarine.' Bergman explained gravely. 'The other is a personal gift from myself.' He leaned closer and lowered his voice confidentially. 'It is one of the most powerful aphrodisiacs ever produced in the Orient - in Japan they call it *Geisha Dust.* Next time you are in bed with a woman ...' he whispered the rest of the sentence into Castilho's ear and the captain giggled.

Bergman waited on the foredeck and watched the boat's crew pulling back to the *Delgada.* Then with a final shrug, he turned away, grabbed the rail of the conning-tower ladder, and hauled himself onto the bridge.

'Secure for diving! All hands to clear topsides. Full ahead both - trim at thirty feet! Take her down please, *Herr Oberleutnant.*'

U-885 slid smoothly beneath the surface and the Tokyo Torpedo began the last lap of its eventful journey.

An hour later, Bergman returned to the wardroom at the end of his Watch and pouring himself the inevitable cup of coffee, he glanced at the empty space on the shelf.

The little bronze casket containing the ashes of the murdered *geisha* was no longer in its place of honour. Settling back on the leather bench with his coffee, the Kapitanleutnant wondered whether the fine grey dust would bring Captain Castilho the same good fortune it had brought to *U-885* and her crew.

In a different way, of course.

EPILOGUE

The terrible losses suffered by Hitler's U-boats in May 1943 when no fewer than thirty-one were destroyed in the first twenty-two days of the month forced Doenitz to throw every available submarine into the battle. So exactly nineteen days after her return from Japan, *U-885* and her crew left Lorient on her next operational patrol under the command of her new skipper, Kapitanleutnant Helmut Basle. She was sunk by the Canadian frigate *Thorlock* on June 25th in position 31°45'W - 58°09'N while carrying out an unsupported attack on the Halifax-Liverpool convoy *HX-208*. There were no survivors.

Castilho spent his £2,000 bonus in three short riotous months. But, sadly, despite the erotic promise of the little bronze casket, he never found the Kapitanleutnant's wonderful aphrodisiac very successful. In fact, the *capitano* often complained in private that, far from rejuvenating his waning sexual virility, the *Geisha Dust* only brought him out in a rash.

A communique issued from the Fuhrer's Headquarters on July 1, 1943 announced the promotion of Konrad

Siegfried Bergman, formerly commanding officer of *U-885*, to the rank of Korvettenkapitan 'for special services to the Fuhrer and the Third Reich'. The promotion brought with it a new appointment...but that is another story

A LOOK AT: THE LAST COMMAND (BOOK FOUR IN THE U-BOAT SERIES)

The war was entering its final phase and the Allied net was closing ever more tightly round the remnants of the Reich. Now the hunter became the hunted and, as each man was forced to admit to himself that the end was inevitable, it was equally inevitable that each should look to his own salvation.

Korvettenkapitan Bergman knew very well that Oberleutenant Karl Zetterling had something to hide but at a time when suspicion was every man's shadow it was vital to move with the utmost caution. Why did Bergman not want Zetterling to carry out the job he had been sent to do? And what was Bergman himself trying to hide?

With the skill which those who have read Action Atlantic and Tokyo Torpedo will have come to expect of him, Edwyn Gray brilliantly recreates the atmosphere of the deadly battle beneath the waves which Korvettenkapitan Konrad Bergman has waged for four years with unrivaled success. But his last command was to be the most dramatic of all.

AVAILABLE OCTOBER 2018 FROM EDWYN GRAY AND WOLFPACK PUBLISHING

ABOUT THE AUTHOR

AUTHOR EDWYN GRAY specialized in naval writing, and has occasionally written short stories.

Born in London, Gray pursued his education at the Royal Grammar School, High Wycombe. After reading economics at the University of London, he went on to join the British civil service.

Gray began his career as an author in 1953, writing for magazines. His first novel was published in 1969, and he became a full-time writer in 1980.

Printed in February 2022
by Rotomail Italia S.p.A., Vignate (MI) - Italy